This Armada book belongs to:

_____

_____

_____

TRIALS FOR THE CHALET SCHOOL

Elinor M. Brent-Dyer

First published in the U.K. in 1959 by
W. & R. Chambers Ltd., London and Edinburgh.
First published in Armada in 1983 by
Fontana Paperbacks,
8 Grafton Street, London W1X 3LA.
This impression 1984.

Printed and bound in Great Britain by
William Collins Sons & Co. Ltd.,
London and Glasgow.

Dedicated to the memory of
my dear mother

CONTENTS

Chapter 1

"TRUST MARY-LOU!"

"REMEMBER that this is sickness term," Miss Wilson said forebodingly.

Miss Annersley, co-Head of the combined school proper and finishing branch with Miss Wilson, glanced up from the sheet of paper over which she had been frowning. "Why the gloom, Nell? Do you feel it in your bones that we're due for one epidemic after another this term? Not," she added candidly, "that I pay the slightest notice to any of your prophecies."

Miss Wilson shrugged her shoulders. "Trust you to be downright crushing! All I was pointing out was that when we *do* get epidemics, it's nearly always in the Easter term. I can't see why I should be jumped on in such a wholesale manner for such a mild observation." She decided to change the subject. "Hilda, why *are* you scowling like that at the letter you have? Who's written about what?"

"It's this new girl," Miss Annersley replied, picking up her letter. "I'm strongly tempted to wish we'd said a very firm 'No' when her guardian first wrote to us."

"Why?" Miss Wilson demanded, leaning forward and twitching the letter from her friend's fingers. "You told me the lady said the girl was slightly deformed as the result of an accident some years ago, but I don't see why *that* should worry you. The girls won't make remarks about it if that's what you're afraid of. They've all had it well dinned into them that that sort of thing isn't done in this school." Her

7

voice died away as her eyes went down the page of small, neat handwriting. She looked up and the twinkle had left her keen grey eyes. "*Oh!* Yes, that certainly looks like being a drawback."

"What *is* all this?" Rosalie Dene, the school secretary demanded. "What does the letter say? Do remember, you two, that I only came up late last night and this is the first I've seen of any of the correspondence since the holidays."

"This came yesterday morning," Miss Annersley said. "Give it to her, Nell. Read it, Rosalie, and tell us what you think."

Miss Dene took the letter, sat back and read it carefully. When she had finished, she sat in a frowning silence.

"Well?" Miss Wilson asked with some impatience in her voice.

"I don't think it's 'well' at all. In fact, I don't like it. The good lady is vague, to say the least of it." She quoted from memory, "'Owing to the accident of which I have already spoken, I am afraid her mind has become slightly warped.' *That* doesn't tell you much. Does the girl tell lies, lose her temper for nothing, help herself to other people's goods—or what?"

"I should think it might be 'what'," Miss Wilson said thoughtfully.

"But, Nell, that may mean anything," Rosalie protested. "How old is she? Is she our only new girl this term?"

"She is," Miss Annersley said, answering the second question first. "I may say I wouldn't have agreed to accept her, but this lady says that she must go to Nigeria to be with her own girl who is expecting her first baby and wants her mother with her—naturally. They are rather afraid of the effect of the climate on Naomi, and their own doctor advised Alpine air for her. Hence, she is coming to us. As for age, she's sixteen."

"*Hilda!* I thought we'd decided after Yseult Pertwee that

we would never again take a girl over fifteen? I'm sure that's what you all agreed on."

"I know; but it was difficult to refuse. You see, Peter Chester put them on to us. And he made sure by writing to Madge Russell and begging her to get us to make an exception where Naomi is concerned. They've been staying in St Peter Port in Guernsey and he was called in to prescribe for the girl when she had 'flu. He says that it must be a school of some kind, as they seem to be oddly minus relatives with whom she could stay. His own Barbara knows her, and so does Vi Lucy, and they would help her over the first few days. In the circumstances, Nell and I decided that we ought to stretch a point. I may say, nothing on earth would have persuaded me to do it if I'd known of *this* complication."

"No, but you can't exactly go back on your word now. We'll just have to take her and hope for the best," Rosalie said. "Only I do wish this Mrs.— what's the woman's name? —oh, Weldon, of course—had been rather more explicit. As things stand, we haven't a clue just what to look out for."

"Well!" A fresh, ringing voice from the doorway broke into their conference and they all turned with sighs of relief. "What's the matter with you folk? You all look as if you'd just heard that your rich old uncle had died and left all the money he had promised to leave you to form a society for the protection of household pests!"

A cry of "Joey!" rose from the three, Miss Annersley adding, "Don't talk such utter rubbish! Anyhow, you're the very person we want. Come in, take off that enormous wrap you call a shawl and sit down. We need your considered advice."

The newcomer laughed as she entered the room, tossing off the great grey shawl in which she had been closely muffled against the piercing cold of an Alpine January day. "You *do* sound as if you'd come to the end of your tether!" She pulled a chair up to the table and sat down. "Well, I'm all ears. Open your hearts and tell me all!"

The two Heads looked at each other, but Rosalie got in first. "Hilda's accepted a new girl who is slightly crippled as the result of an accident. She's just had a letter from the kid's guardian to say that her mind is also warped—though *how* warped, the lady doesn't condescend to inform her. She accepted the girl before this and now she's by way of regretting it."

"Well, that sums it up very neatly," Miss Wilson observed. "All right, Joey. Rosalie's put the whole thing into a nutshell and you know everything—except that the girl is sixteen, so will be among the Seniors."

"Where among the Seniors?" Joey demanded.

"VIb, to be exact, so I suppose it isn't quite so bad as it might have been."

"I see." Joey considered a moment. "In VIb, you say? Who does that consist of at the moment?"

"Your English!" Miss Annersley murmured with an air of deep pain.

"Never you mind my English. Much more important to try to solve this latest problem. Rosalie, you keep the registers. Who, exactly, is in VIb now?"

"Oh, Verity Carey, Barbara Chester, Josette Russell, Prunella Davies, Jessica Wayne, the two inseparables, Christine and Catriona. How many is that? There are twelve of them, all told. That lot, anyhow," Rosalie Dene replied.

"There'll be thirteen of them, if Naomi goes there," Miss Wilson remarked.

"Is that her name? Well, I don't see any reason to worry about any new girl warping the minds of any of that lot. Every one of them is a girl with a mind of her own."

"I'm not worring about that so much," Miss Annersley said slowly. "As you say, that crowd all have minds of their own—even Jessica. At the same time, they have important public exams ahead of them and I don't want them upset."

"It'll all depend on the kink in her mind, won't it? May I see the letter?"

10

Miss Annersley passed it over to her and she settled down to read it while the other three watched her anxiously.

When she had finished, she looked up. "Ye-es! It does leave you rather hung up, I must say. This may mean anything. What are you going to do about it?"

"That's what we're considering," Miss Annersley said. "Have you any ideas?"

"Give me a chance! I've just this moment heard your tale of woe. I'll give you one idea, though. Turn Mary-Lou on to her."

"How do you mean?" Miss Annersley demanded.

"Just what I say. Look, Hilda! Mary-Lou is the sort of girl you can take into your confidence. Furthermore, she may be only seventeen in years, but as we all know, mentally, she is considerably older than that." She glanced round them with questioning eyebrows and they all nodded assent. She went on; "She has her head well-screwed on and she *is* extraordinarily understanding. On top of all that, she is *kind*. If you take my advice, you'll explain things to her—a little, anyhow. At least give her some idea of what to expect. Then, you can leave it to her. She'll cope all right, or I don't know my Mary-Lou!"

"I don't think I like it," Miss Wilson said after a moment.

"What don't you like about it?" Joey demanded.

"This is Mary-Lou's last year at school. I know she's coming on to St. Mildred's for a final year, but it's not the same thing. Once she finishes here, she is no longer a schoolgirl. She's Head Girl this year, which gives her plenty to do in any case. I don't think it's fair to dump a heavy responsibility like Naomi on her at this stage."

"But, my dear Bill, you know as well as I do that May-Lou *thrives* on responsibility! Heaven knows she's butted in over and over again when no one asked her to!"

"Oh, we all know that Mary-Lou has inherited your mantle—"

"Rosalie Margaret Dene, may I ask what you are talking about?"

"Josephine Mary Maynard; you may. You, let me remind you, were the school's prize butter-in—still are, if it comes to that. Mary-Lou is just a chip off the old block in that direction."

"She's no such thing!" Joey said heatedly. "I suppose I *might* have been her mother, but I'd have had to start jolly early in that case! The girl's nearly eighteen!"

"So she is. But I didn't mean that way, but—well, *spiritually*. At the same time, I agree with Nell that it's rather hard lines to ask her to take on any special effort now. She told me at the beginning of last term that she meant to enjoy this final year at school. She has no exams to bother about and she's specialising in her own subjects. Ordinary Head Girl duties she can take in her stride. If we turn her on to a girl with warped tendencies, that's going to be an extra job. She'll take it on if she's asked, of course, but are we being fair to her?"

Joey looked thoughtful. "You know I'd forgotten how nearly Mary-Lou's school career was at an end. Oh, dear! There are times and seasons when I wish children didn't grow up so rapidly. Look at my triplets! Fourteen last November—into their fifteenth year and in the Senior school! And it seems only yesterday that they were tiny girls, trotting everywhere after Mamma."

"Bless me, you've plenty of babies to go trotting round after Mamma still, haven't you?" Miss Wilson demanded. "There are Felix and Felicity. Cecil's on her feet now. You aren't left babyless. And if I'm any judge of the matter, it'll be a few years yet before you have *that* particular loss to growl about."

Joey grimaced at her. "I hope so! I *like* long families!"

"Well, you've *got* one—nine is a long family all right!"

"Ten, when July comes," Joey said calmly. "That was my real reason for dropping in on you now. Only I may as well

12

tell you that Jack and I are hoping for twins again, so that will make us eleven."

"Joey Maynard!" The shriek came from three voices.

"You're incorrigible!" Miss Annersley cried. "Anyhow, this isn't getting us any further with Naomi—"

"Yes, I was going to ask you," her co-Head interrupted her. "Are we to speak to Mary-Lou or not?"

"I shall have to consider it before I say anything. Oh, I daresay I shall agree in the end. For one thing, quite apart from her influence over other girls, I don't see anyone making much impression on *her* mind. Mary-Lou has a tremendous personality and she will stick to her own lines. But I can't say now."

Joey, her news announced and her advice given, stood up and picked up her shawl. "I must fly back. The family is making toffee and fudge and there's only the Coadjutor in charge, this being Anna's free day. As for putting Mary-Lou on the job, you must make up your own minds about that. But I'll say this. Whatever you do about it, if there's anything outstandingly odd about this new girl, you can trust Mary-Lou to spot it and wade in on her own. I think you might as well leave it at that, now I come to think of it. She'll see to it, whether you do anything or not. And what's more, if she does, you can trust her to make something out of the poor child. Now I'm going!" And with that, she departed and left them to make up their own minds as she had said.

Chapter 2

A JOB FOR MARY-LOU

THE Chalet School—or such of it as came from any distance, which means most of it—was arriving for the new term. As usual, they had left the train at Berne to pile into the big motor-coaches in which they made the last stages of the journey up to the Görnetz Platz, high in the mountains of the Oberland Alps. After a wide detour across the plain, there had been the long climb up the road which was originally built for the passage of motor ambulances to and from the great Sanatorium which stood at the far end of the Platz. Now they were running smoothly along, past tiny villages, perched among the mountain slopes and the pines, between the walls of the mountains, beyond solitary chalets and huts built here and there in niches.

The leading coach carried the members of the two top forms. As they were all girls of sixteen and over and had all the prefects with them, they were without any mistress. This was a much-prized privilege, for it meant that speech could be free. Even the best of mistresses, as Clare Kennedy of VIb remarked, could cramp your style on occasion. The Seniors and mistresses, especially the younger mistresses of the Chalet School, were on friendly terms as a rule, but it *was* a joy to be able to gossip as they pleased and not to have to pick and choose their English!

Seated at the back of the coach was the Head Girl, Mary-Lou Trelawney. She was a tall girl, very good-looking, with a mass of silky golden-brown curls clustered tightly over her

14

shapely head, clear blue eyes and a glorious complexion. However, handsome though she might be, character was not lacking in her face. Her short chin was firm and there was a look about her finely-cut lips that told you that when Mary-Lou chose to dig her toes in, she was a very hard nut to crack!

On her right was Hilary Bennet, another tall girl, with a head of boyishly-cut wavy hair and a piquant face of her own. On her left was Vi Lucy who, so far as looks went, beat most of the others hollow with her bronze curls, deep violet eyes and perfect features. One either side of this trio sat Doris Hill, an ordinarily pleasant-looking girl, and Lesley Malcolm who had no claims to beauty, though her keen, clever face stood up well to the contrast with the centre three.

These five formed the backbone of the prefects and, as anyone in the school could have told you, Mary-Lou was their leader in most things. They had spent most of the long journey from England in exchanging news of their holidays. Now that school was so near, Mary-Lou saw fit to change the subject.

"Winter sports this term! And, thank goodness, they seem to have had plenty of snow."

"*And* a good hard frost," Doris Hill supplemented. "I'm aching for it. I was frightfully disappointed with last term."

"Oh, we hardly ever got much in the Christmas term," Vi told her. "January, February and March are the best months for winter sporting."

"I'm looking forward to a gorgeous term," Mary-Lou added.

"You'd better touch wood," Lesley warned her seriously. "It doesn't do to be too optimistic."

"Why, what do you expect to happen that's so awful?"

"Nothing in particular; but I don't believe in tempting Providence," Lesley replied, laughing. "And why more gorgeous this term than usual?"

"Well, think of it—no exams to worry about; I *think* I can manage the Head Girl business all right, now I've got into the way of it; nothing in the shape of out-of-school extras, since the Sale's been shifted to the summer term. The pantomime is St. Mildred's affair and won't affect *me* this year. In fact, I expect to be able more or less to sit back and enjoy life for once."

"Yes; it does look as if it might work out like that for us," Lesley owned.

"Apart from the usual bothers with the Middles," Doris warned them.

"Oh, surely we've got all that well taped by this time?" Vi said.

"You can *never* have Middles 'well taped'," Mary-Lou asserted. "They think up the maddest things that no one in their senses would think of forbidding until the little pests have done them."

"Well, you ought to know!" Josette Russell, sitting beside Barbara, told her with a grin. "I never heard that *you* crowd were a bevy of little angels when *you* were Middles. I know *I* wasn't!"

"Oh, Middles are all alike for that," Doris returned, rather sweepingly. "I'll tell you what I'm so thankful for and that is that we're all specialising now. I do find that a most terrific relief!"

"By the way," Vi observed, "didn't Biddy O'Ryan—I mean Courvoisier—say that she wasn't coming back this term? We'll have a new history mistress, then. I wonder who she is and what she's like?"

"She won't come up to Biddy," Lesley said positively. "It will be very difficult for anyone to take *her* place. I'm on the science side as you know, but I wouldn't have missed one of Biddy's lessons for anything you could mention."

"Nor I," Vi agreed. "Anyone else after her will be a fearful drop."

"There's Freudesheim!" Josette suddenly exclaimed. "Look! Auntie Joey at the gate to welcome us! Oh, I wish they'd stop the coach and let us have a word with her." Here, she waved wildly at the window. "I've heaps of messages from Mummy for her, and a whacking big parcel."

"The Head will let you go over tomorrow some time," Mary-Lou said soothingly.

"I know that." Josette sat down as the coach swung round the wide curve and the gate of Freudesheim was out of sight. "But I'd like to see the twins and Cecil for a moment. The boys will all be back at school now. They start earlier than we do; but I'd like to see the babies."

"The Trips will be at school and you can see *them*," Vi grinned. "You pipe down, Josette."

"She'll have to, anyhow," Doris said as she peered into the gloom. "We're turning in at the gate this minute."

It was a very short drive and they could all see the light pouring out into the darkness of the January evening from the wide-open hall doors. Lights gleamed in many of the windows, too. At the doors stood the two Heads to welcome them back, those of the staff who had not been on escort duty standing behind them, and further in, clusters of girls, mainly those who lived on the Platz or in the Swiss towns and cities, for the Chalet School, which had begun life as a cosmopolitan school but had lost it when it had been forced to leave Tirol, the place of its birth, was now regaining its old position and almost half of the girls there now were not British.

Another moment, and the motor-coach had pulled up before the four shallow steps which led up to the building. The girls hurried to claim their hand luggage and scramble out. The cases were all deposited on a big truck beside which stood Gaudenz, the man-of-all-work. Then the big girls swept forward and streamed into the house to be greeted warmly by the two Heads before they passed on to line the walls, standing in close ranks. Everyone must be squeezed in somehow, and already the girls from Vb and Inter V were following on their heels.

It was more than a squash, as Doris, standing next to

Lesley Malcolm, murmured; but they managed it. By the time the last Junior had been crowded in and the staff, laughing gaily, were standing on the stairs, everyone had been pushed into line somehow and the big doors were shut.

"Welcome back girls!" Miss Annersley said, her beautiful voice ringing clearly across the phalanxes of girls all looking at her as she stood on the bottom stairs. "I won't talk now. Abendessen is ready and I'm sure you are, too. Go off, form by form to your Splasheries and get rid of your outdoor things and change your shoes. When the entire form is ready and *not before*, march to the Speisesaal and take your places quietly. You may talk till the gong goes. Then be silent, please. Lead on, there, second form!"

The little girls marched off smartly at once, the rest following to their cloakrooms which were always called Splasheries. The prefects went last and as Mary-Lou passed her, Miss Wilson, standing near the corridor leading to them, touched her on the arm. The girl stopped at once.

"Yes, Miss Wilson?" she queried.

"When you are ready, Miss Annersley wants to see you in the study, so be quick, please."

"Yes, Miss Wilson." It was all Mary-Lou said, but her blue eyes were like saucers. This was *not* in accordance with the general rule.

"Tell Vi Lucy to take over for you until you return—but it won't be for more than a minute or two. Now fly!" Miss Wilson turned away with a smile and Mary-Lou scuttled off after the rest.

"What did Bill want?" Vi demanded as they hung up their coats and berets and fished in their lockers for the house shoes left at the end of the previous term.

"Not knowing, can't say." her friend replied airily. "I've to go to the study when I'm ready. The Head wants me. Am I decent?"

"You're all right—except your hair. That's a bit wild. Run

18

a comb through it and then you'll do," Vi said as she took a hasty look at her friend.

Mary-Lou obeyed and then with a quick, "Take over, Vi, will you?" fled to the study. She tapped at the door and went in quietly at Miss Annersley's summons, remembering to pause long enough to make her curtsy. When the school began, Miss Bettany as she then was—Lady Russell, these days—had adopted certain Tirolean customs and manners and the courteous salutation to the Head was one that had never been omitted.

Miss Annersley was standing behind her desk. She smiled at her Head Girl before she said, "You have been quick, Mary-Lou. I won't keep you, dear. I'm sure you're longing for Abendessen! We have a new girl this term—Naomi Elton. She is a senior and will be in VIb. I want you take charge of her for the moment. You know what to do." She turned to an armchair standing with its back to the room. "Naomi, come here, my dear. This is our Head Girl, Mary-Lou Trelawney. She will look after you for the next day or so until you begin to feel your feet. Mary-Lou, Naomi knows Barbara Chester a little, so put her to sit next to Barbara."

"Yes, Miss Annersley," Mary-Lou replied, inwardly wondering why Barbara had not been sent for in the first place.

"Thank you, dear. That's all I want now. Go with Mary-Lou, Naomi."

Naomi had been getting slowly to her feet and now Mary-Lou found herself looking down on a girl who was badly stooped with a crooked shoulder. But the face lifted to hers was lovely—almost as lovely as Vi Lucy's with cloudy fair hair framing perfect features. Dark grey eyes looked straight into hers as Naomi said, "How do you do?"

It was a musical voice, but there was a hardness about it which rang in Mary-Lou's ears at once. The perfectly cut mouth was set in thin lines and there was a crooked twist to the smile which accompanied the words.

"Hello, Naomi," she said, with her own delightful smile.

"Come with me and I'll see you through. So will Barbara."

She led the way to the door where she paused to curtsy, then she ushered the new girl out, thinking to herself that perhaps Lesley had been right to warn her to touch wood. She felt an odd repulsion to the girl mixed with the genuine pity that rose in her warm heart for anyone so terribly deformed.

Chapter 3

NAOMI

"THIS place is a regular rabbit warren for corridors," Mary-Lou said as she tried to match her swinging walk to Naomi's halting progress. "It used to be a winter-sports hotel, you see, and a bunch of chalets and pensions nearby. It's all linked up with covered passages on the ground floor now, but it does make it something of a day's march to get from one end of the place to the other. However," she added cheerfully, "you'll soon get to know the geography of the place. And while I think of it, this is first day when rules are more or less in abeyance. From tomorrow morning onwards, no talking in the corridors or on the stairs unless it's absolutely necessary—and you've got to satisfy the powers that be that it *is* necessary, or else!"

Naomi flashed a quick look at her. "Or else—what?" she asked, pausing a moment and leaning against a set of shelves as if she were tired.

Mary-Lou glanced at the stick on which she leaned, and stood still. "Was I going too fast? Sorry! Why didn't you yank me back before?"

"It's all right, I'm just a little tired. I flew here this afternoon," Naomi said, resentment plain in her face. "Go on and tell me about the rules."

Mary-Lou was wise enough to let it go. "Oh, if you talk out of turn, so to speak, you're fined, that's all."

The delicately arched eyebrows drew together in a quick frown. "I thought a breach of rules would mean an order mark or lines or something like that."

Mary-Lou shook her head. "Order marks are mainly for untidiness or cheeking the prefects and it's mostly Juniors and Middles that go in for that sort of thing. Talking in forbidden places and at forbidden times always means a fine."

"I see." Naomi began to limp forward again. "Certainly, I must avoid leaving my things about and cheeking people. One hardly wants baby punishments when one is verging on the adult stage, does one?"

Mary-Lou was, for once in her life, silenced. There was a nasty little undercurrent in Naomi's voice which made her wonder. When she spoke again, it was about the fines.

"Of course, you're fined, too, if you forget to use the set language for the day. That can mean that when the end of the week comes, you're penniless. *Not* a very pleasant state of things, for you mayn't borrow or anticipate your weekly allowances except for church collections or stamps. Here we are!" as they turned a corner. "Down this corridor. Here's our door. The staff use the one further up." She nodded towards a second door in the wall, then opened the first and led the way into a long, narrow room, bright with lights, gay cloths, coloured glasses and pretty tableware. There was a steady hum of laughter and talk mingled with the sound of knives and forks at work. Abendessen had begun already. Mary-Lou took Naomi to the table where the prefects sat in all their glory. Her quick eyes noted a vacant chair between Barbara Chester and Prunella Davies, and she led Naomi to it.

"You sit here for the moment," she murmured. "You'll have to say your Grace to yourself. We're too late for ordinary Grace." Then she left the new girl and made her way up the table to her own seat at the head, where she sat down and bent her curly head for a moment as she murmured her Grace.

Naomi stared, but she fell in enough with Mary-Lou's ideas to bow her own head in the same way. When she raised it, someone was setting a plate of meat before her and Barbara was pushing a dish towards her, filled with tiny golden potato-balls.

"Hello, Naomi," she said pleasantly. "I didn't know you were coming here. Have some potatoes and then give the dish a shove on to Mary-Lou, will you?"

Naomi helped herself and passed the dish on. Someone offered her a sauce-boat of rich, delicious gravy; her glass, after a question as to whether she would prefer milk or lemonade, was filled with rich, creamy milk and she was able to begin. Mary-Lou had not waited for her. She was tucking in at a tremendous rate, being, as she plaintively remarked, famished by this time.

Presently, when the edge was taken off her appetite, she smiled down the table at Naomi who was eating in much more deliberate fashion, and began introductions in the breezy way that seemed habitual with her.

"Everyone! Meet Naomi Elton who has come to grace our sixth forms. She's in VIb. Naomi, the person on my left is Hilary Bennet who is games prefect. On my right, our second prefect, Vi Lucy—"

"I know Vi," Naomi interrupted her. "We met when I was staying in Guernsey."

Vi nodded pleasantly at her, though her eyes were clouded. Mary-Lou glanced at her questioningly, but said nothing. She merely carried on with the good work. "Next to Vi—Barbara Chester, her cousin. You know Barbara, too, don't you?"

"Yes; we have met two or three times," Naomi replied distantly.

"And on your other side, Prunella Davies, who is your form prefect."

"When did you come?" Prunella asked. "I didn't see you on the train."

"I flew with Aunt Harriet," Naomi replied. "It's quicker

23

and, they thought, easier for me. I'm a cripple, you see." Her lips twisted as she spoke.

Prunella was silenced, but Hilary picked up the ball and tossed it back.

"Flew?" Her saucy, laughing face wore a frankly envious look. "Oh, lucky you! I've always longed to fly but Dad says he isn't a millionaire and I can wait for such luxuries until I can provide them for myself."

A tall girl with the face of a thinker who was sitting on the other side of the table, glanced at the Head Girl with a wicked smile. "Remember when you asked the Head if we should all fly to school, Mary-Lou?"

Mary-Lou hid her face in her table-napkin while the rest shouted.

"Lesley, you wretch!" she said when she emerged again. "Shall I ever be allowed to forget that historic occasion?"

"Never!" they assured her in a laughing chorus.

"And," Lesley Bethune continued in a meditative voice, "when the Head asked you if you had any idea what it cost, you replied, "Not a sausage!" Even Miss Annersley had to laugh on that occasion!"

"All the same," Vi interrupted her, "she sat very heavily on your little aspirations. And if you're going to give Naomi all our names, you'd better stop reminiscing and get on with it."

"So I had. The next one to Vi is Doris Hill, Naomi, and next to her," she projected a smile at the small, slight girl in that place, "is my sister-by-marriage, Verity Carey."

Naomi was taken off her guard. "Your what?" she jerked out in the ordinary tones of any schoolgirl.

"Sister-by-marriage. Her father married my mother when we two were Senior Middles. We aren't step-sisters, so that's what we call it."

"Oh, I see." Naomi looked across at Verity, whose small-ness made her seem almost out of place among the elder girls.

"Welcome to our midst," Verity said in the silvery voice

that seemed to match both her size and her amazing fairness. Indeed, if it had not been for her eyes, she would have been almost insipid; but those glorious eyes of vivid gentian blue, with finely arched brows and long lashes of black prevented that.

Mary-Lou grinned to herself and went on with the introductions. The girls all spoke to the stranger pleasantly and when Mary-Lou had finished, she summed up the position with her usual clarity.

"Well, now you know our names. You'll soon learn which to fit to which person if you don't remember now. Barbara, you'll give Naomi a hand? She's in your form, so take her to stationery and the stockrooms tomorrow, will you, and see that she gets everything she needs."

Barbara nodded. "I'll see to it. I'll make out the list as soon as I can, Naomi, and come and help you collect them."

"Thank you," Naomi said. "I'm afraid I could hardly carry much myself. Being a cripple means that one is able to do so little of that sort of thing."

The girls glanced at each other uneasily. It was difficult to know what to say. Naomi knew it quite well and her eyes gleamed as she saw their discomfort. On the whole, it was as well that the maids arrived to change the plates and by the time they were all busy with a delicious creamy mixture, the moment had passed and Mary-Lou had changed the subject.

When the meal was nearly at an end, a bell sounded from the high table. At once the chatter and laughter ceased as the girls turned in their seats to face up the room to where Miss Annersley, very trim and attractive in her blue woollen frock, had risen.

"After Grace," she said, "clear the tables, please, and then go straight to Prayers. After Prayers, Juniors and Junior Middles go to bed. Everyone else will go at their usual time. That is all at the moment."

She sat down and the girls went on with their meal. When it finally ended, they all stood, each girl stepping to the left of

25

her chair before pushing it in to the table. Naomi, slower than the rest because of her lameness, waited until her neighbours had moved before she fumbled for the stick she had laid beneath her seat. Mary-Lou, seeing her difficulty, was at her side in a moment, but her help was repelled freezingly.

"Thank you, but I can manage for myself. I am not entirely helpless," Naomi said as she slowly levered herself to her feet with the aid of the stick.

There was no more to be said. Mary-Lou, flushing, went back to her seat and the new girl stood behind her chair, her fair hair bent as decorously as anyone else's, while the Head, in the beautiful voice that Joey Maynard always declared was one of her greatest assets, repeated the short Latin Grace they always used. The staff followed her out of the room, but some of the prefects hurried to the back where several trolleys were standing and brought them up to the tables in turn. Others were already passing plates, cutlery, glasses and dishes up to the top.

Meanwhile, the rest had seized on their napkins and marched off to place them in a drawer of a great armoire that stood at one side. Two other people, swept and folded the cloth and added it to the drawer before it was closed. Naomi, still standing by her chair, nearly gasped. The entire room had been cleared in exactly seven minutes and the girls were forming into two lines near the door. Then Mary-Lou was once more at her side.

"Prayers now," she said. "Are you Protestant or Catholic?"

"Why?" Naomi demanded.

"The Catholics have Prayers in the gym. If you are Protestant, you go to Hall." Then, as the new girl stared at her, she added somewhat impatiently, "Of course we separate for Prayers! What else did you expect?"

Naomi gave that curious, twisted smile of hers. "I can't really say *what* I am. Aunt Harriet could never make up her mind, so sometimes we went to the Church of England,

26

sometimes to Chapel and sometimes to the Catholic church. It all depended."

"Depended on what?" Mary-Lou asked involuntarily.

"On what sort of music there would be or the preaching and so on. Some Sundays, we didn't go anywhere, of course."

"But what am I to do with you?" the Head Girl cried. "Weren't you baptized anywhere?"

"Not that I know of." Naomi replied calmly. "My people were agnostics, I believe, and Aunt Harriet thought it better to try everything before I made up my mind."

Mary-Lou stared at her speechlessly. This was a problem she had never run up against before. There *had* been girls who didn't care in the least about religion, but even they were nominally members of some form of Christianity. There was only one thing for it. She must go to Miss Dene who would surely have some idea as to which branch this odd girl was to belong—for belong to one or the other, she must, so long as she was in the school.

"We'd better go to the office," she said slowly. "I don't suppose you'll be allowed to run from one to another as you choose and you'll certainly not be allowed to stay away from either Prayers or church. Everyone goes. I expect your aunt will have told Miss Dene which she wants you to attend." She looked down at Naomi and added, "It's getting frightfully late. I think you'd better wait here, while I fly—" Miss Dene herself interrupted this speech, coming into the Speisesaal in search of her handkerchief which she had dropped.

"What are you two doing here?" she asked. "You ought to be at Prayers."

"I know," Mary-Lou said. "The thing is, which services is Naomi to attend?"

"Church of England, my child. Mrs Weldon said she had better attend them for this term, anyhow. Next term, she is to consider and decide for herself." She gave the new girl a curious glance. Already this fiat had caused a hubbub in the

27

staffroom, for such an arrangement had never before been heard of at the Chalet School. Then she turned back to Mary-Lou. "You go ahead, Mary-Lou. You ought to be in your place now. I'll bring Naomi along with me. Off you go!"

Mary-Lou nodded and left the Speisesaal, going with long, swift strides. As she went, however, she wondered to herself what sort of home the new girl came from. In her experience, you definitely knew where you stood in religious matters while you were at school.

"It strikes me that Naomi is going to be a weird sort of problem," she said to herself as she turned in at the top door of Hall and went to take her seat. "But I'm awfully sorry for her. She has a big load to carry with her lameness and, apparently, she hasn't anything to fall back on but herself."

"Where on earth have you been?" Hilary murmured as she sat down. "Here's your hymn book and Bible and I've found the parable of the Talents for you. What have you been doing to be so long in coming?"

"Tell you later," Mary-Lou murmured back. "Thanks for finding my place."

There was no time for more, for the bell rang and instant silence fell as the mistresses came in to take their places. Miss Lawrence, head of the music staff, was already at the piano and had been playing softly. Now as the Head came to stand before the carved oak lectern, she struck a chord and the girls all stood to sing the beginning-of-term hymn. The clear voices rang out through the great room, for everyone who could sing, sang with all her heart. Naomi, standing listening, wondered a little. She wondered more when Mary-Lou stood out and read in a clear, steady voice, the parable of the Talents. For the first time in her life, the young pagan found herself listening and taking it in. Perhaps the shock the Head Girl had just received caused her to read it with more than usual emphasis. However it was, Naomi was struck by the fine old story and when they all knelt to pray, she was startled anew by the air of devotion around her. She realised that

Prayers meant more than a mere form to most of these girls. For the first time, she was moved to wonder what it was like to be so sure of help and comfort. Then she shook herself. She didn't believe in it and she could think of nothing that was likely to make her believe.

All the same, when the others rose from their knees and she sat back in her chair—kneeling was out of her power, of course—she found herself wondering about it all through the brief words the Head spoke to the assembled school when the Catholic girls and staff had come in and taken their places with the rest. She tried to laugh at herself for being so impressed, but it would not do. Already, she was feeling the influence of the Chalet School.

Chapter 4

A PUZZLE FOR VIB

BY Monday, the two Sixths were in a complete state of bewilderment over Naomi Elton. She was totally unlike any girl they had ever met before. Quite a number had been attracted to her at first by her face which, in both features and colouring, were almost perfect. They were sorry for her lameness and her crookedness, but they knew better than to say anything. Apart from the fact that it had been well dinned into them from Junior days that personal remarks were not only ill-bred, but also unkind, there was something about the new girl that forbade any show of pity or sympathy.

She had gone to Prayers with the rest without further demur. On Sunday, when the Protestants all attended their own service in the little chapel about a mile along the road, she had been drawn there by Mary-Lou and Vi, who had tucked her and her stick and the prayer-books of all three on a toboggan, and, themselves on skis, had pulled her along. It had been a gloriously fine day with a bright sun and no wind, but bitterly cold for all that. Naomi, well wrapped up in her fur-lined coat and big scarf, felt the keen air stinging her face. Everyone had been warned to wear tinted glasses against the glare of the sun on the snow. As Miss Annersley had reminded them at Frühstück, snow-blindness can be most unpleasant.

"What, exactly, *is* snow-blindness?" Naomi had asked.

She was answered by Emerence Hope from Vb. "Oh,

simply awful! You see everything through a red, swimmy mist. I know! When I was an ass of a kid, I took my glasses off one day and I had a sweet three days or so of it as a result. I've never played *that* trick again, and don't you risk it, either, Naomi."

"Not being an ass of a kid, I shall certainly not do it," Naomi said sweetly; and Emerence went red.

She sat through the service with a queer, half-amused, half-scornful expression on her face. Only when they sang did it vanish. Verity Carey was at one side of her and she was the owner of a really lovely mezzo-soprano voice. As her clear, larklike notes went soaring up, Naomi's eyes glowed unexpectedly. She was not singing herself, but she gave her full attention to Verity's singing.

Needless to state, her absorption had not passed the Head Girl. That eagle-eyed young person, sitting on the other side of the aisle, watched her in the intervals and nodded to herself shrewdly. "Music means something to her," she thought as they sat down after *Jerusalem the Golden*. "That may very well be a key to her make-up. I must remember that. For she really is the oddest creature I've ever come across!" Then she turned her attention to the sermon.

In the afternoon, most of them went for walks. Naomi was told that it was too cold for her and she had better find a book and stay quietly in the common room. Two Juniors who had complained of toothache the day before were also staying and so was Marie Zetterling from Va who had twisted an ankle during the holidays.

Mary-Lou was all prepared to go with the rest. There was nothing she liked better than a ski-run in weather like this. Then she saw Naomi limping along to the common room by herself, while everyone else in the Sixths was heading for the Splashery to get ready. She watched that proud, lonesome figure and a queer look crossed her face. The next moment saw her heading for the stairs.

31

"Where are you going, Mary-Lou?" Hilary demanded at the sight.

"To fetch my book and writing-case," Mary-Lou told her firmly.

"What? Oh, don't talk rot! You're coming out with us, aren't you?"

"Not this afternoon. I haven't finished my letter home and Mother will be expecting it by the usual post. I can't disappoint her."

"But you've plenty of time after Kaffee for that," Hilary protested. She was a nice girl, but she was lacking in insight. "If you come to that, I haven't finished my own screed home. Give it a miss and come along, do!"

"Not today. I have to write to Clem, too, and I haven't done much more than a page and a half to Mother. You trot off and leave me to go my own way."

Vi, who saw beneath the surface far more deeply than Hilary, glanced at her friend and then along the corridor where Naomi was making her uneven progess to the common room.

"I'm staying, too," she said quickly. "I've finished my letter to Mummy, but I've got to write to Julie and I want to send a line to Beth, as well. Hang on a sec, Mary-Lou. I'm coming to bag my things, too."

"Idiots!" Hilary commented heatedly. "Tomorrow we may wake up to a minor blizzard and there'll be no going out. Surely those extra letters can wait a day or two more? Oh, come *on*, you two, and don't be asses! It's a glorious afternoon for a run. Let the letters go hang!"

"Clem's can't!" Mary-Lou retorted. Then she added rather more gently, "It was this week that the news came that her father and mother were dead and she still feels miserable about it then. A letter from me full of school gossip helps her. She says so. I can't let her down in those circs, can I?"

Hilary flushed. "Oh, in that case, I'll say no more. Give

Clem my love and say I wish she was back here still. But *you* could let Julie and Beth wait, Vi."

Vi laughed. "And have Julie going up in the air at me for not writing? No, thank you!"

"Have it your own way! I think you're a fuggy pair. I'm off to enjoy myself in the great outdoors!" Shrugging her shoulders Hilary turned down the passage to the Splashery and wriggled into coat, scarf and beret and went off with some of the others. It was not until bedtime that enlightenment came to her. Then she wished that she had thought of it herself.

Meanwhile, the other two, having secured their novels and writing cases, descended to the common room where they found Naomi seated in a chair near the tall white porcelain stove, staring into space.

"Haven't you anything to read?" Mary-Lou said as she dropped her belongings down on a nearby table and began to lug it nearer the other girl. "You can take any of these, you know." She waved her hand in a lavish gesture towards the low shelves that ran round two sides of the room and were loaded with books to suit every taste. "These are our own— sixth form books, I mean. They don't belong to anyone else and only we may borrow them. Got any special likes, Naomi? Shall we help you find something before we get down to our letters?"

Naomi gave herself a shake and got up slowly and painfully. "I can manage, thanks," she said. "I know I'm lame, but I *can* get about. You go on with your letters and pray don't trouble about me."

The two prefects glanced quickly at each other and then looked away again. Neither knew what to say in reply to the bitter little speech. Naomi was at the bookshelves now, her back turned to them. Clearly, she meant what she said. They pulled up their chairs, sat down and began to write.

It was a silent party in the common room. Naomi, having chosen her book, sat hunched over it, taking no notice of the two prefects. They scribbled industriously but only part of their minds was fixed on what they were doing. They were all too conscious of the waves of dislike the new girl was spreading round them. What made it worse was that neither could think what she had done to deserve such feelings.

Later, at Kaffe and Kuchen, which on Sundays the two Sixths had in their own common room, more than one of the girls tried to talk to Naomi. She made little attempt to respond and her dry, nippy replies to their remarks made them draw off in the end, so that she was left to sit in silence while the gay chatter of the rest flew round her.

Most of the Seniors went to Evening Service and Mary-Lou, feeling that in giving up her walk, she had done her share for one day, departed with them. Only Naomi of the two Sixths was left, and Miss Dene, finding her sitting alone in their common room, promptly shooed her off to join the dozen or so Fifth formers who had also remained at home.

"You can't stay alone here," she said briskly. "Besides, there's no need to burn extra electric light for one girl only. Come along Naomi. You'll find plenty of company in the Fifth form common room."

Naomi went reluctantly. She would far rather have been left alone. Miss Dene handed her over to Richenda Fry of Vb who happened to come along the corridor at the same time, and then went to fulfil her promise to read some of *Swiss Family Robinson* to the younger girls.

"Come along in and sit down," Richenda said amiably to the new girl.

Naomi glanced at her with a frown, but she did as she was asked without comment.

"How do you think you'll like it here?" Richenda asked.

"I have scarcely been here long enough to find that out. Do *you* make up your mind to your likes and dislikes in three or four days?"

Richenda felt snubbed, but she was a good-natured girl, so she tried to find some other topic that would interest this very odd new girl. After having tried three or four only to have each wet-blanketed, she gave it up. Jo Scott, the prefect of Vb then took a turn, but she was no more successful than Richenda. It ended in Naomi being left to herself for a while.

Towards the end of the period, two more girls came to speak to her—Jocelyn Fawcett from Va and Joan Baker of Vb. Jocelyn was a girl who was curious about everything. Joan had proved herself a real problem for the school. Indeed, during her first term, she had come within an ace of being sent away. She had improved in some directions, but bad early training allied to a feather-headedness that was inborn, had made it difficult for anyone to have a great deal of influence over her.

These two began asking questions about Naomi herself. She endured it for a short space. Then she struggled out of her chair. Leaning on her stick, she looked them over with an expression in her eyes that made them feel queerly uncomfortable. At last she spoke.

"I had no idea," she said icily, "that in a school where the girls were *supposed* to be gentlewomen—at least, I imagine so—people would be so totally incapable of anything approaching real conversation." With which she limped off to the door and vanished, leaving them staring after her in consternation.

Monday saw the beginning of full school rules, among them, the one that made German the language for the day. Mary-Lou had carefully explained this to the new girl the evening before when they were sitting in their common room after Prayers.

"You see, we are all supposed to learn to be fluent in French and German when we come here," she said. "We speak German on Mondays and Thursdays; French on Tuesday and Fridays; English on Wednesdays and Saturdays. That gives us all a fair chance. When we first came, of course, most of us were English. Now, we have at least as many continentals—French, Swiss, German, even

35

some Dutch and one or two Italians. This school is regularly cosmopolitan! Can you speak either French or German, Naomi?"

"Oh, yes," Naomi said carelessly. "We lived in Vienna for a year once, so I picked up quite a good deal of German then. French, I know even better. I shall get on all right, I expect. It's exceedingly kind of you to be so solicitous" she added with a drawl, "but really, there's no need, you know. I have a very good brain—perhaps to compensate me for my other disability."

It was just as well for her that this unpleasant speech was made in private. Mary-Lou was a tremendous favourite in the school and it would not have endeared Naomi to anyone if they had overheard her biting snub in return for the Head Girl's kindness. Mary-Lou took it in her stride. She did wonder what she could have done to set the new girl so much against her, but she merely replied, "Oh, then, that's all right. But if you get stuck and I'm anywhere in the offing, ask me. Or any of the others, either," she added.

When she was in bed that night, she thought it over. "Poor kid," she said to herself. "Probably she's frightfully sensitive about her lameness and is afraid of being criticised or laughed at. As if she need fear anything of that kind *here*! Just let me catch anyone doing anything of that sort and I'll make her wish she had never been born!"

Naomi came to lessons with a superior air that made everyone else in VIb ruffle up like a set of young turkey-cocks. They were not accustomed to that sort of thing in new girls who, as in most other schools, were expected to be on the *piano* side for the first few weeks, at any rate.

As the morning went on, they found that she had every reason for her superior airs. Her maths were as good as those of Virginia Adams and Jessica Wayne. Her German was excellent, even colloquial, and her accent drew a commendation from Miss Denny who taught it. She had been well taught in geography and when it came to history, the other members of VIb found that she could reason from cause to effect and vice-versa as well as they. A new mistress, Miss Charlesworth, had come to take the place of the beloved Miss O'Ryan when that lady discovered that she would be unable to go on teaching, now that she was married. Much to their relief, they found that Miss Charlesworth taught history along the same lines, though it must be owned she lacked the flow of picturesque language which had so enlivened the now Mme Courvoisier's lessons for them.

It was another fine day, so after Mittagessen and their afternoon rest, no one was surprised when Miss Burnett, the games mistress, arrived in Hall to announce that, apart from the art classes, everyone was to go out for ski-ing, tobogganing or generally playing about on the meadow they usually used.

"What about us, Miss Burnett?" demanded Len Maynard of Vb. "Have we to go to the art room as usual while everyone else is winter sporting?"

Len sounded deeply injured and Miss Burnett gave a chuckle before she replied blandly. "And why not? Herr Laubach has come up for your art classes. You surely don't expect him to forego them?"

Several faces fell noticeably at this dictum and the mistress indulged in yet another chuckle before she relieved their minds. "As a matter of fact, he is taking you to the meadow to practise snapshot sketches.. Take your blocks, pencils and rubbers and the sketching-stools in case you need them." Then she swung off and they were left to pack up their deckchairs and cushions before heading for the Splasheries to get ready.

Chapter 5

Two Violent Tempers

MARY-LOU was on her way out of Hall after seeing to the stacking of the deckchairs they had been using for the half-hour's rest, when Barbara Chester went scuttling past her in search of her block and pencilbox. The Head Girl caught her arm and pulled her up short.

"Half a sec! Have you seen that Naomi has everything she needs? Or hasn't there been time yet?"

"Saw to it on Friday," Barbara replied. "In fact, I've made jolly sure she has everything—including all she wants for art. I say, Mary-Lou, how do you think she'll get on with Herr Laubach? I should say she has a nasty temper when it's roused, and you know what *he* is!"

"She may have a gift for it," Mary-Lou said hopefully.

"And she may not! In any case, no matter how much of a gift you have, he can always find something to rage about. Look at the way he raves at Vi!"

"We can't do anything about it, my lamb. We must hope for the best."

"And prepare for the worst. I get you. One other thing. How is she to get to the meadow? She doesn't ski, of course; and walking will be the edge today!"

"Oh, that's easy. Vi and I are tobogganing this afternoon. We'll park her on the toboggan and pull her there. No; don't go yet. Just see to it that everyone has all she ought to have with her, will you? We may as well keep the old boy as sweet as we can," Mary-Lou said with feeling. "Remember, you're art prefect and it's your job."

38

"O.K., Grannie! I know it all too well."

They parted on that note. Barbara went flying along to Vb's Splashery to demand a show of all art materials and find out that Mary-Lou's warning had been well justified. At least half the girls were proposing to go without some vital belonging. Mary-Lou scurried off to the prefects' Splashery where she dressed in short order, talking hard in German all the time to Vi Lucy. Then she left her friend to go and seek the toboggan they usually shared while she hunted up Naomi, intent on giving her the invitation.

Naomi was in VIb Splashery. Prunella Davies was helping her with the great shawl that was a *must* when they had to do any sitting or standing about in cold weather. Mary-Lou waited until it was properly folded, and arranged so that it covered back and chest. Then she nodded to Prunella, who went off to attend to herself.

"I was looking for you, Naomi," she said in her friendly manner. "I know you don't ski. Walking is appalling when the ground's frozen like this. Vi and I thought you might like to ride on our toboggan. We can pull you along and it would be doing us a good turn if you would. Your weight would steady the thing, you see. It's always more of a nuisance if you have to haul it light ship, so to speak."

Naomi's brows had been drawing together; but at the new expression, they straightened, and she said, "'Light ship?' What *do* you mean?"

"Oh, haven't you heard it before?" Mary-Lou said airily. "That's what they say of a ship that puts to sea without any cargo. Well, will you come, Naomi?"

"You will if you know what is good," Josette Russell, standing near, observed. "You wouldn't like a second passenger by any chance would you, Mary-Lou?"

"Not if it's a lump like you!" Mary-Lou retorted. "OK, Naomi. We'll be waiting for you outside the side door. I must fly!"

She left the Splashery, intent on seeing that the long lines of girls were in some sort of order. Naomi, left with the others, discovered that she was envied.

"Lucky you!" Josette said in Geman.

"Isn't she?" Christine Vincent chimed in. "Are you sure you're well wrapped up, by the way? Standing about doing snapshots isn't a very warming business on a day like this."

Naomi glanced at her. "I am quite warm, thank you," she said. Then she added, "You all seem to make yourselves very busy about other people, especially Mary-Lou."

"Well, that's one reason why she's Head Girl," Christine said.

"Really? How very interesting. She certainly seems to attend to that part of it *con amore*," Naomi said suavely, picking up the light bag containing her art materials and slinging it over one arm before she took her stick.

In their indignation at the covert sneer, no one noticed that she had taken the wrong one. She had two—one with a rubber ferrule for the house; the other steel-pointed for such times as this. The one she took now had the rubber ferrule. She limped off out of the Splashery, followed by Josette Russell, who was also ready. On the way, Josette wondered to herself if she ought to say anything about the new girl's attitude to Mary-Lou. Then she decided against it. It really was no business of hers, and it was hard to see how she could begin. Better leave it to Mary-Lou herself. Naomi would soon find that the Head Girl's kindness was genuine and not put on. "And that," thought Josette, "is more likely to make her think again than anything I or anyone else could say."

Miss Wilmot, head of mathematics was in charge that afternoon, though, as everyone knew, every single mistress who could manage it would be at the meadow. She was a plump, pretty young woman, easy going to a degree, though she had her limits as sundry people who had presumed on her knew all too well. She smiled at the two girls as they arrived in the doorway, and nodded at them.

"Naomi, I understand Mary-Lou and Vi are taking you

along to the meadow on their toboggan. Josette, if you and the rest of VIb who are here like to get off, you may. Go straight to the meadow, and mind you stick to the road until you're there. Herr Laubach will be waiting, and I know he wants to start you all as soon as possible.

"Oh, thank you, Miss Wilmot," Josette said, her face lighting up. She fell in with the half-dozen or so of her form who were already waiting, and they skimmed off gaily.

Miss Wilmot turned to Naomi. "Take my arm, Naomi, and I'll lead you to your chariot. The ground is like polished glass today." She tucked Naomi's free hand through a strong arm and brought her to where the two prefects, very trim and smart in their ski-ing suits of gentian blue with caps, gloves and scarves of crimson, stood waiting.

"Here's your passenger!" she cried as they came near. "Give me your bag, Naomi. And your stick. Ease her down, Mary-Lou. There you are! Here's your bag! All quite safe? Good! Then you three had better be off before the crowd come. Take her to Herr Laubach, you two, and see that she has a sheltered corner. *He* won't think of it, and the wind has a bite today, even though it was sunny all the morning."

"But there's no sun now," Vi pointed out. "Just as well, too, considering the art crowd. I can't imagine snapshotting through coloured specs."

"I know. But if the clouds break, be sure you put your specs on," Miss Wilmot returned as she left them for the next job, dismissing them from her mind.

"You all right?" Vi asked as she stood to her rope.

"Quite, thank you," Naomi replied.

"Then off we go! Ready, Mary-Lou?"

The two prefects set off at once. They were on skis at the moment, and Naomi, sitting helpless on the toboggan, fiercely envied their free, graceful movements as they skimmed over the glassy surface, drawing the toboggan easily and steadily. What would she not give to be able to move like that! Why should other girls be free while she must go limping through life, always heavily handicapped?

Her face became sullen as she sat behind them, scarcely answering their chatter. Why should she have suffered that horrible accident which had left her the twisted thing she was? Of course they pitied her, these girls! They dared to pity her, she who had as good brains as anyone in the school; whose beauty was unmistakable—and here, she spared time to hate her unmarred beauty and wish that the fire which had caused her lameness had rather scarred her face and left her to move freely.

"Why should they be so happy?" she thought bitterly as their laughter rang out at a quick sally of Mary-Lou's. "I hate them! I wish I could spoil their fun! I wish I could make them feel as miserable as I do! They'd know all about it then! They mightn't laugh like that if they'd ever known what it is to be so handicapped. And I'm young; not yet seventeen. I may live another sixty years, a crippled thing like this! Oh, I *hate* them!"

They reached the meadow, where they left the road, and the two prefects, after a quick glance round, drew the toboggan to the big bush where Herr Laubach, the art master, was already busy, instructing Josette in the need for economy of line in snapshot sketching. While Mary-Lou carefully helped Naomi to her feet and gave her her stick, Vi went up to him with a note the Head had asked her to give him. He scanned it swiftly and nodded his great head.

"Very well," he grunted in his native German. "I will remember. And what about you, hein? You do not sketch today?"

"It isn't our lesson today," Vi said hurriedly. She was one of the few girls in the school who usually escaped a bad tongue-lashing from him, for she had a real gift for art. All the same, she had no idea of giving up her fun for one of his lessons. She hoped Mary-Lou would hurry up with Naomi, or he was quite capable of sending her back for her materials and insisting that she join his lesson. For really gifted pupils, he spared no pains. For those who were mediocre or poor, he never spared his tongue. Vi was moved to hope that he would handle Naomi gently. Otherwise she could see sparks flying!

Mary-Lou, who had welcomed her release from all art lessons at the end of the previous summer term with cries of joy, put Naomi's stick into her hand, and then turned to Vi.

"We ought to be getting to the top of the run, Vi. I can see the others coming, and we ought to be up there before them. Otherwise, there's no knowing what mad things some of those young monkeys from the Fourths may do."

"I'm coming," Vi said, blessing her friend mentally for this tactful speech. "You'll be all right now, Naomi. Herr Laubach will look after you."

The master raised his eyebrows as he noted that she addressed the new girl in easy German. "You speak German, hein?" he rumbled at Naomi.

The prefects were already off before they could hear her reply that she could. "Das ist gut!" he grunted. Then he went on to ask what she had done previously and what her training had been. By the time he had settled her in the lee of a bush, the others were arriving, and soon the meadow was crowded with girls flying here and there or, in the case of the novices, finding that skis have an unpleasant habit of crossing their points before you have gone very far and sending you over.

Naomi was seated on a campstool, and having started her off on making—or trying to make—sketches of the others, he turned to attend to someone else. The other members of VIb had also arrived and were standing about the edge of the ground, doing their best to produce snapshots of the rest. Naomi saw that they were allowed to move now and then. Only she was glued to her stool.

Herr Laubach came to her now and then to criticise her drawing, and he found plenty to criticise. Clever in most other ways, Naomi was no artist, and before long the art master's hair-trigger temper betrayed him. Snatching her block from her, he ripped off the sheet on which she had been trying to reproduce something of what she saw, crumpled it up, and almost threw the block back at her with the furious comment, "Wooden—*wooden*—WOODEN! They do not move! They are blocks—puppets! Look you!" as Mdlle de Lachennais, doyenne of the staff and head of the languages, flew past with a lovely swooping movement. "Mark the curves of the figure! See how she uses the arms—the sticks! Begin again and drew me *people*, not *dummies*!" With a final furious grunt, he went off to reduce Heather Clayton to the verge of tears by even unkinder criticisms, leaving behind him a seething Naomi.

In her rage she forgot her helplessness. Seizing her stick, she forced herself to her feet. The rubber ferrule failed to grip on the icy ground. She staggered, made a wild effort to recover her balance and fell headlong, striking her head on the icy snow, and stunning herself completely.

Chapter 6

A TRIAL FOR MATRON

IN the end, though Naomi came to herself in the school San with an outsize in headaches and a lump like a cricket ball on her brow, it was poor old Herr Laubach who was the greater sufferer. He blamed himself bitterly for losing his temper with the girl, and finally demanded an interview with the Head during which he requested her to accept his resignation for the end of that term.

Miss Annersley was greatly distressed. Herr Laubach had been at the shool from its beginning. Joey Maynard always referred to him as "one of the more important foundation stones." When the Nazis had marched into Austria, he had delayed escaping only because he had an invalid wife. After her death he had seen her decently buried, and then left the country by a devious track, arriving at the school practically penniless. There he had been ever since.

"Oh, Herr Laubach," the Head said anxiously, "*must* you? Frankly, I do feel that Naomi herself is chiefly to blame for this accident. If she had not been careless enough to take the wrong stick out, it might never have happened. And you are one of us—have been with us so long. We can't spare you. Do change your mind and stay! I know Madame would say the same thing."

"If I had ever learned to control my temper, also it might never have happened," he said sombrely. "Listen, gnädige Fräulein! You must not disturb yourself for me. I am an old man, now—too old to change my nature. I have enough

45

saved to live in quiet comfort. The school has been very good to me all these years, and now I have no one but myself to keep. Yes; I am old—sixty-six this year. It is time I retired and left the post open for a younger man. So, I will go."

"Sixty-six is *not* old nowadays," Miss Annersley said firmly. "And the girls do so well with you generally."

"Ah, well, let us say, then, that my age, he is not old, but I myself am. The old pepperpot is growing too old and too peppery to teach these present girls. So I will go. But not far. The school is my whole life now, and I will find me a chalet up here where I can see you all and visit you. Perhaps, even, some of you will visit me. But no longer will I teach. No, no; that is over for me when this term ends."

Miss Annersley argued in vain. She even sent Rosalie Dene flying across to Freudesheim to bring Joey to back her up. It was no use. He had made up his mind to retire, and retire he would. Between them the three got him to agree to finish the year, but when the summer term ended, his teaching must end.

"I could cheerfully take that wretched girl across my knee and give her a little of what she deserves!" Joey declared wrathfully when he had finally stumped off. "I'm raging mad! Poor old Herr Laubach!"

Miss Annersley had been thinking it over. "Yes; I know how you feel. But I'm beginning to think that perhaps he is right. He has worked hard all his life, and it is time he rested now." Then she smiled. "He has paid us a wonderful tribute, Joey. He says the school is his life and he will not go far. Think what that means, coming from Herr Laubach! Well, we must see about finding a chalet for him and as a farewell gift, the school shall see that he has every comfort."

"*Comfort!*" Joey echoed. "My good Hilda, we shall pretty well have to *furnish* it for him! He lost everything when he fled to England before the war. He's lived in rooms ever since. I doubt if he so much as owns a chair, a table, and a bed! But as for a chalet, short of *building* one for him, I don't know where

46

you'll find one up here! Every hole and corner is chock-a-block, these days."

"You never know what may happen," Rosalie said hopefully. "We must keep our ears and eyes open, and, the first chance there is, snaffle the place at once. We have the best part of six months for it, Joey, and that should give us time to find something."

"We can *try*," Joey said sceptically, "but I doubt if we'll succeed." On which note she departed homewards, still very indignant.

Naomi remained in San four days. By that time her head looked more or less normal, and she was as well as usual. Matron, who never stood any nonsense, then told her that she was quite well enough to be at lessons, and returned her to school. But the Head sent for her, and gave her a sharp rebuke for her carelessness in the matter of the stick before informing her that, in future, she need not attend any more art classes.

Naomi remained expressionless during the interview, but inwardly she raged. However, she had enough sense left to keep her feelings to herself, and when she was dismissed, she went to VIb, outwardly her usual self. None of the other girls had been near enough to know exactly what had happened, and she kept her own counsel. Neither, of course, did they know that the episode was to be the reason for the severing of Herr Laubach's connection with the school as art master.

Herr Laubach himself made pitiful efforts to control his temper in lessons. He succeeded to some extent, thereby giving the girls a shock. Never had they known his criticisms of their work to be so mild, and Vi Lucy, for one, was certain he must be ill!

The next trial that came, however, was a very different matter and one that gave the entire school something to think about.

It began with Margot Maynard, the youngest of Joey's triplets. She woke up one morning in a bad temper, and throughout the day behaved as if she had a whole kennel of black dogs on her back. She even quarrelled with her bosom friend, Emerence Hope.

"What's eating you?" Emerence demanded when she had been flatly contradicted three times and snarled at into the bargain. "You're acting like a bear with a sore head today. Got out of bed the wrong side? Come off it, Margot, and be your own sunny self! You're like a thunderstorm and a blizzard rolled into one!"

"Oh, shut up!" Margot flared. "I'm sick of all your silly talk!"

Emerence got up from her seat beside her friend with some dignity, gathered her possessions together and marched off to another seat with her head in the air. Margot remained hunched up over the cane basket she was weaving—they were at a Hobbies meeting—and snapped at everyone who merely asked her to pass something. As a result, by the end of the evening everyone was giving her a wide berth, and she stamped off to bed at war with her entire world.

In the middle of the night Matron, sleeping peacefully, was roused by an agitated knocking at the door. She was out of bed and pulling on her dressing-gown and slippers, even as she bade whoever it was to come in. Emerence entered, looking alarmed.

"Please, Matron," she said, "will you come to Margot? She's frightfully hot and her eyes are all shiny and funny, and she's talking the most awful rot."

"No slang!" Matron snapped, opening a drawer and bringing out her thermometer. "And why, pray, have *you* come to fetch me? I thought Penelope Grant was dormitory prefect there? Aren't you in Daisy? Margot is in Pansy."

"I know; but Penny was sent for on Saturday to go to Berne to see her people, and she's not back yet. Carmela Walther is sub-pre, and she was scared and came for me as we are next door. She said Margot had wakened them all up with talking."

By this time, Matron was ready. She hustled Emerence out of the room, snapped off the light, and then led the prefect of Daisy down the long corridor until they reached the open doorway of Pansy. Margot's voice could be heard, pitched a full tone higher than usual and running on in an excited way which told Matron plainly enough that something was badly wrong. She paused before she went in.

"Have you been bending over her, Emerence?"

"Well, I had to," Emerence said apologetically. "I tried to get her to see sense, but she didn't seem to know me, and she was so frightfully hot—*burning* hot, in fact. I guessed she was running a temp, so I came for you."

"I see. You haven't been back in your own dormitory, have you?"

"Oh, no. I just came straight for you."

"H'm!" Matron thought a moment. "You'd better go straight to San and rouse Nurse. Ask her to get a bed open and a hot bottle in it, and stay and help her. Don't go anywhere else until I've seen you again. Run along."

Emerence "ran along", and Matron, with a strong feeling of coming trouble, stalked into the dormitory where all the lights were on and a mumur of voices told her that the girls were all awake.

"Everyone into bed at once!" she said. "Carmela, are you with Margot?"

The curtains of Margot's cubicle parted, and Carmela Walther, a gangling, mop-headed creature with eyes like blue saucers, appeared. "She was trying to get out of bed, Matron," she said anxiously. "I thought I'd better stay and try to keep her in."

"Very sensible of you; but now you may go back to your own. I'll see to her. Be quick about it! It's a cold night!"

She left Carmela to attend to the matter, and went on into Margot's cubicle, arriving just in time to see that young woman fling off the bedclothes and begin to get out. Most

49

unexpectedly, Betty Landon from Vb was with her, and Betty was trying to push the younger girl back on her pillows.

"And what are *you* doing here, may I ask?" This was Matron at her grimmest.

Betty turned a frightened face to her. "I heard someone run past our door, so I got up to see what was happening. I didn't see who it was, but the light was glaring out of here, so I came along and found Margot like this."

"I see. Well, you'd better wait here. I shall need help, I expect. Let me see."

Betty stood back, and Matron stooped over Margot. There was no mistaking it. She was running a high temperature already, and rising almost every minute to judge by the signs. Matron opened her pyjama jacket and scanned her chest. What she saw there made her mouth come down. She buttoned up the jacket, and sent Betty flying to fetch Nurse and the light stretcher that lived in San.

"Matron, is it—is it something—infectious?" Carmela ventured.

"That's for the doctor to say when he comes. May just be tummy upset. We must wait and see," Matron replied. "Meanwhile—do you hear me, all of you?—no one in this dormitory is to leave it for any reason whatsoever until I've been round in the morning. Is that quite understood?"

"Yes, Matron!" It came in two or three languages and the meekest of voices. Matron on the warpath was not to be argued with. In fact, no one had ever dared to defy her for long, and Emerence Hope, who had tried it on in her very early days at the school, could have told them that the consequences were far too unpleasant for it to be worthwhile!

Meanwhile, Matron was continuing her examination. Margot's pulse was racing and her rapid mutterings never ceased. Her skin was dry and her blue eyes were brilliant with fever. Matron finally drew back just as Betty returned with Nurse and the stretcher.

The two people most responsible for the health of the

school conferred briefly. Margot was rolled in blankets, laid on the stretcher, and Betty summoned to help Nurse carry her along to San. Matron remained. She had something to say to the people in Pansy.

"Girls! Which of you are in Margot's form? And which sit near her at table?"

"Me," said a meek voice from the next-door cubicle. "And Zita, and Penny, when she's here."

"Oh, yes; Penny's in Berne, isn't she? H'm!" Matron said, speaking more to herself than the girls. "That's a nuisance!" She raised her voice again.

"Prudence—it *is* Prudence Dawbarn, isn't it? I thought so!" As Prudence assented, "Well, can you tell me if Margot has been off her food at all?"

There was a pause. Then Prudence said, "Well, she played a lot at Frühstück. I did notice that."

"Why didn't someone report it to me?" Matron asked sharply.

"We thought she was just in a bad temper," another voice replied in Italian.

"Is that Zita Rincini? What do you mean—in a bad temper?"

"Well, she was," someone said from the far end of the dormitory. "Most of us have had our noses snapped off today by her. And she didn't do a thing at lessons."

"Janet Kemp, is that you? How was she during Hobbies this evening?"

"Worse than awful!" Janet replied fervently. "She even fought with Emmy Hope."

"She has been cross—oh, but *so* cross all day." This was a French girl, Marie Lemprière. "Truly, Matron, we have left her to herself she was so cross."

"I see. Then that is all. Lie down now, all of you. I'll send some hot milk round presently and then you are all to go to sleep and no more talking. I shall come back later, and I'll see anyone I catch talking or out of bed in the morning."

51

With which dire threat, she rustled out of the dormitory and left them to obey her.

She went straight to the school San, where she found Margot already in bed. Nurse glanced up as Matron came in and gave her a look which brought the elder lady swiftly to the bedside. Margot's jacket was open again, and already a telltale rash was beginning to show on her chest. Matron inspected it, and then, as Nurse tucked the patient up firmly, she moved away from the bed to the window where Nurse joined her a minute or two later.

"Scarlet, I'm afraid," she said softly. "I've sent Betty to ring up Dr. Graves and Carmela to the extension off this room to get Mrs. Maynard."

"What? Joey can't come here! She has the twins and Cecil to consider."

"I know that; but she ought to know. Wasn't Margot the delicate one of the triplets?"

"She was; but that's a thing of the past, thank goodness! What have you done?" She nodded at the bed where Margot seemed to be quieter at the moment.

"Gave her a cooling mixture. That won't hurt, whatever it is. But it strikes me we'd better face the fact that we're more than likely in for a raging epidemic. Scarlet can be infectious, you know, in the early stages."

"Don't I know it!" Matron groaned. "And where she's got it from, I can't think."

However, that problem was solved by Dr. Graves when he arrived, which was an hour later. He had been out when Betty put her call through, summoned to the small son of a visitor, who was undoubtedly down with scarlet fever. The children at the Görnetz Platz were apt to be together a good deal during the school holidays, and Matron, answering a call from a frantic Joey, soon learned that the boy had played most days with her family.

"And do you realise what *that* means?" Joey wound up. "My own three lads are back at school, and ten to one they'll hand the wretched germ all round. Jack must ring up first thing in the morning to warn the folk there. And Matey, when can I come and see Margot?"

"Not at all," Matron returned promptly.

A loud wail answered her. "Matey! I simply must!" Then her tone changed. "There's Cecil again! She's cutting one of her double teeth, poor pet, and having a bad time of it. And Felix is inclined to be whiney. Tummy, I think—"

"Where's Jack?" Matron cut her short ruthlessly. "Felix whiney? Use your sense, Joey! Hasn't he been exposed to infection as much as the boys or the triplets? You dig Jack out and ask him to look at Felix at once! I'm going. You can ring me after Frühstück. But unless I'm much mistaken, Felix is starting scarlet as much as Margot." With which she rang off.

So she never heard till next day that Jack Maynard was at the great Sanatorium at the end of the Platz and not available when Joey heard the news. However, that young woman took no risks. She rang up until she got hold of a doctor, and for her pains was told that in all probability Felix was infected as badly as his sister, and she must keep an eye on Felicity and Cecil into the bargain.

"And considering all things," Miss Annersley remarked when she heard the news. "I think we'll have to do something about it. Joey must *not* be left to cope unaided with anything like that. I'll go and consult Matey and Nurse."

Chapter 7

SCARLET FEVER

THE awful news had to be broken to the school next morning. Dr. Graves had diagnosed Margot's illness as scarlet fever almost as soon as he set eyes on her. By the time day was breaking, the rash was coming out all over, though her temperature had dropped a point or two, and when she roused from an uneasy sleep, she was sensible enough. He warned both Matron and Nurse, however, that she would probably go up again as the day wore on, and they were in for a hard two or three days of it. Her throat was badly inflamed, and when Nurse asked if it had been sore at all, she croaked that it had felt "rough" for a day or two, but she had said nothing as she didn't want to miss any fun.

She was in no state to be scolded, but Nurse afterwards owned that it would have been a relief to give her a good shaking! Jack Maynard came home at last, and once he heard Joey's news and looked at Felix who was decidedly cross and complaining that it hurt to swallow, he bounded across to the school to interview the authorities.

"We're in for it," he told the three who organised affairs. "That wretched Johnson child is well away with it, and he's spread it—not a doubt!"

"Then," Matron said firmly, "there's only one thing to do."

"What's that?"

"We can isolate properly, now we've built on to this place. I propose that if any of the outside children—including the

54

Johnson boy and your own Felix—start, they come to us. You must get us nurses up from Berne or Lucerne or somewhere. We'll turn the San into an isolation hospital. If need be, we can use one of the houses—St. Hild's would be best as it's next the San—and with any luck we ought to be able to confine it fairly closely to the Görnetz Platz."

"She's right," Miss Wilson said. "What's more, once any of the two Sixths can be released from quarantine, they can come along to St. Mildred's. I hope we shall escape altogether and it would make things easier for you folk. Now, what's the next item on the programme? Find out who has had it before, I suppose."

"I doubt if more than a dozen or so have had it," Miss Annersley said gloomily. "I thought it was almost wiped out, these days. Well, we'll just have to face the fact that practically the whole school may go down with it. All right, Gwynneth." She turned to Matron. "We'll ring the bell and get them all into their form rooms, and you and the other matrons can go the rounds. What will you do?"

"Take temps and look out for sore throats and general poorliness. Jack, you'd better get off and let the outside families know what we have decided. And above all things, do what you can about getting us extra help. We'll *need* it!"

The staff were interrogated first. Only three knew that they had had it in their extreme youth. Miss Ferrars acknowledged to a sharp attack when she was a Kindergarten baby; and Miss Andrews and Miss Wilmot had also been victims. The rest were sure they had never met it or else had to find out from home.

By the time the girls had all been examined and had replied to the question, "Do you know if you have ever had scarlet fever?" the school hummed. The Juniors were examined, but not questioned, older sisters answering for some while parents had to be asked about the rest. By the time the last reply had been received, there were two rooms full of cases in San, among them Joey's twins, Hilary Graves' small

Marjory, and the two elder children of Dr. Morris, who was on the Sanatorium's staff. Forty-one out of the almost three hundred girls had definitely had it. Twenty-seven more were doubtful. The rest all had to be closely watched.

Joey Maynard, arrived three days after Margot began, and held an anxious conversation with Miss Annersley through the study window, having been forbidden to set foot inside the school buildings.

"Cecil seems all right so far," she reported. "*And* the tooth is through, thank goodness! How are the rest of my family?"

"The twins are cross and whiney, but theirs are light cases. So far, Len and Con are all right. Margot's temp is down and *staying* down at last, thank goodness! But she's very weak, poor little soul, after all that fever. Any news of the boys?"

"Oh, Mike's got it." Joey said resignedly. "I expect Charles and Steve will follow suit. What the school must be saying about us, I shudder to think!"

"They'll get over it," Miss Annersley said philosophically. "There's one mercy."

"Oh? Whats that? So far, I don't see any mercy about it at all."

"Oh, but there is! Scarlet isn't anything like the awful thing it used to be. The really tiresome side of it is that it's so lengthy—six solid weeks. However, we can't help it. Thank Heaven Jack got us extra help!"

By the end of the week the school San was packed, and one dormitory in St. Hild's had been requisitioned. Matron had the rest of the house cleared out, and the girls were packed away in odd holes and corners. Twice a day temperatures were taken, and in three weeks at least half the school was down and most of the small fry living around in the chalets. But, thanks to the measures taken by the school, the disease was confined to the Görnetz Platz.

"And what about our exams?" croaked Josette Russell as, wrapped in a blanket, she was borne off to St. Hild's.

"Mercifully, you ought to be over this by half-term, and

you'll have the second half and all next term till June to prepare," Miss Ferrars told her unsympathetically. "Anyhow, Josette, if you aren't ready now you ought to be. Stop fussing!"

"I did hope I'd escape!" Josette wailed.

"Well, you haven't, but you're going to be a very light case."

"I feel rotten enough now," Josette informed her. "My throat is *sore*!"

"Then stop talking and give it a chance to rest!"

Matron had issued an edict that no one was to be allowed to feel sorry for herself, and anyone who tried to bid for pity was briskly treated.

"What's happening to the St. Mildred crowd, I wonder?" Mary-Lou asked of the thinned-out Sixth form common room during the last week of quarantine.

"I can tell you that," Hilary Bennet said. "So far, they haven't had a single case. If they keep all right, they're going down to Unter die Kiefern until the place is clear. What's more," she added, "any of us who escape are going down with them. There's glory for you, my sweetiepies!"

"How do you know?" Vi demanded.

"I was in the office helping Deney to sort the correspondence, and she told some parent or other over the phone. She knew I was there, so she obviously didn't mind my knowing, and she said nothing about keeping it to myself."

"Well, it's something to look forward to, anyhow," Mary-Lou allowed.

"Where is Unter die Kiefern?" Naomi asked. This past week or two had done something to turn her thoughts away from herself, and, as Vi had remarked only that morning, for her, she was becoming quite chatty.

"It's the shelf below this," Mary-Lou explained.

"St. Mildred's used to be there. But it gets frightfully hot in summer, so they were moved up here, and the house was turned into a kind of hostel for people who came to see any of us or had friends or relatives along at the big San."

"It's where they had their first panto," Hilary said. "I say! I never thought of that before! What do you think will happen about this year's?"

"It's a fortnight past the date," Vi said. "I suppose they'll have to wait until all this mess is cleared up, and have it then."

"It's a good thing our Sale was moved to the summer term," Lesley Malcom remarked. "Someone at the door, Mary-Lou."

"Come in!" Mary-Lou called; and Len Maynard came in, followed by Con.

"Hello! What do you two want?" the Head Girl demanded.

"Deney's gone to bed with a smashing headache, and the second lot of mail has just arrived," Len began. "The Head wondered if some of you Seniors would go to the office and help sort it. Anyhow, she asked us to come and ask you."

Mary-Lou jumped up. "Of course we will! Come on, folks!"

Vi got up slowly. "I'll come with pleasure. But I wonder . . ."

She stopped there, and the others, including the two Maynards, stared at her.

"What are you getting at?" Hilary demanded.

"Well, the staff have gone free, so far," Vi said.

"Oh, my only aunt! Are you suggesting that some of *them* are coming down now?" Mary-Lou demanded.

"It's quite likely, isn't it?" Prunella Davies, who had sat silent so far, pointed out. "They've been in as much infection as we have, haven't they?"

"I never though of *them* getting it," Lesley observed. "But you're quite right, Prunella. Oh, my goodness! What's going to happen if many of them go down?"

"What happened last year when we had that 'flu epidemic," Mary-Lou said.

"It was the year before," Hilary corrected her. She projected a grin at Con Maynard, who was standing listening with brown eyes as wide as pennies. "What price Daniel in the lions' den, Con?"

Con, went scarlet. "No one will ever forget that. And it wouldn't have happened if I hadn't been thinking of something else."

"To wit: a poem," Mary-Lou said teasingly. "All right, Con. You aren't the only one to provide howlers in this school, though I'm bound to say that was one of the loveliest I ever heard." She gigled as she remembered it. "Meanwhile, ladies, may I remind you that the mail awaits our attention? Come on, whoever is coming, and let's get to work and stop nattering."

"All the same," Len said. "it's time that silly yarn was dropped. I daresay if I think round I can remember quite a few things other people have said—older people than us, I mean."

After this, feeling that she had said enough, she gave Con a tug, and the pair slipped past Lesley at the door, and went scuttering off before anyone could call her to order.

"She's right," Mary-Lou said as the six or seven girls who were the sole representatives of the two Sixths at present, followed their juniors down the corridor, en route for the office. "Con's been teased enough about that old howler, and those three aren't really kids any longer now."

"What *did* she say?" Naomi asked curiously as she limped along beside Vi.

"Oh, the Head asked what happened when Daniel was in the lions' den and Con, who was in a dream as she frequently was in those days, said Daniel bit the lions," Vi replied with a giggle.

Naomi stared. Then, for the first time, her laugh rang out, startling the other girls considerably. It was such a very pretty laugh, bubbling up like a spring and rippling happily along. It was pure mirth and some of them laughed in sympathy. Mary-Lou jumped, and then glanced round sharply at her. If Naomi could laugh like that, why in the name of everything that was queer did she usually condescend to give only that sarcastic smile as a rule?

By this time they were at the office door, and saw the Head sitting at Miss Dene's desk, fishing out the great bundles of letters from the postbag. She looked up with a smile of welcome.

"What, all of you? Then this will be quickly done. Take charge here, Mary-Lou, and let me have all my own letters as quickly as you can. Typing is not an accomplishment of mine, so I shall have to answer what I can by hand."

Hilary came forward eagerly, "Miss Annersley, I can type—I taught myself on Daddy's old portable. Couldn't I do some of them for you?"

The Head had been going through the connecting door into the study. Now she stopped short, and looked at Hilary. "That's an idea, Hilary. Could you really manage, do you think? For, apart from what you can do for yourselves, I'm afraid you girls are going to be short on lessons for a while."

"Oh, are some of the staff down?" Mary-Lou asked anxiously.

"Yes; though I'd like you to keep it to yourselves for the moment. Miss Derwent certainly has it, and so has Miss Moore. Matron took them both over to San after Mittagessen. And I'm very much afraid that this headache of Miss Dene's is the forerunner of an attack, though her throat is still clear."

"Well, you'll let us help out, won't you?" Mary-Lou implored. "We VIa people have no exams to worry about, so we could help with the lower forms, couldn't we? And if Hilary can type, she can help in the office."

For the first time almost in her life, certainly since her accident, Naomi was moved to offer to help someone else in a difficulty. "I can type, too, Miss Annersley. If you have another typewriter, I could give Hilary a hand with some of the letters." Then she stopped and marvelled at herself.

Miss Annersley looked round at them all with shining eyes. "You dear girls! We'll be only too glad of any help you like to offer. It won't be for long—can't be! Your quarantine ends this week, and if you remain all right, we shall pack you off to Unter die Kiefern until we're declared free from infection. But if you *could* take hold for the next day or two until we can get things rearranged, it would be a tremendous help. I accept your offer with gratitude. You see, the only mistresses we can be fairly sure about are Miss Ferrars, Miss Wilmot and Miss Andrews. None of the others seem to have had it. Now Miss Derwent and Miss Moore have set the example, I'm just afraid that some of the others may follow."

"We'll help—we'll be glad to," Vi declared. Then she added diffidently, "That is, if we can. You won't ask us to take Va, for instance, will you?"

The Head laughed. "No; Va can look after themselves. But you could take the Lower Fourths for dictation in all three languages, and French grammar and a few things of that kind, couldn't you, Vi?" She turned to Naomi. "Naomi, if I agree to letting you help with the typing. I want your promise that you will stop if it makes your back ache, my dear. In fact, if any of you feel headachey or backachey, you are to report at once. Thank you very much, girls. This will solve quite a number of problems. Naturally, we can't import temporary staff at the moment."

She left them to it after that, and they sat round the table, sorting the letters and packages into forms, the staffroom, the domestic staff, and above all, the Head's share, which made up at least a third of it all.

"Poor Abbess, if she's got to look through all that lot!" Hilary said as she picked up the fat bundle. "What a blessing Daddy let me mess about with that aged affair of his when I wanted! I don't pretend to be very quick, but I can be

61

accurate, which is something. What about you, Naomi?"

"Oh, I'm just moderate," Naomi replied. "But with two of us, we should manage quite a lot. Which is this packet for, Mary-Lou?"

"The two Upper Fourths," Mary-Lou said. "That's the lot done! Come on; we'll go and find out what our several fates are to be."

Thereafter, all the well members of the Sixths found themselves well and truly occupied. As Miss Annersley had feared, the mistresses began to fall before the foe, and by the end of the week seven of them were in San in addition to Rosalie Dene. She was the only one to cause any anxiety. She had not been too well before the epidemic began, and for a day or two they were very anxious about her. Then the obstinate temperature broke and danger was over, though she remained terribly weak for some time to come.

By this time all the Sixths had been marched off to Unter die Kiefern, where they joined the St. Mildred lectures and rejoiced in former friendships renewed with gusto among the girls who had gone on the previous September. This lasted for another three weeks or so, by which time most of the early patients were quite recovered and making up for lost time by devouring enormous meals and asking for more. Then, when only the mistresses who had gone down were left as inmates of the isolation rooms in San, Matron had a grand disinfecting of the entire school, followed by a thorough cleaning, and at last the girls came back.

"I suppose we may be thankful it's been no worse," Miss Annersley said wearily to Matron late that night. "St. Mildred's have escaped all through, thank goodness, and even Margot is convalescing most satisfactorily."

"*And* Naomi Elton has escaped," Matron added briskly. "I'm glad of that, I can tell you! What's more, she seems changed a little. She gave me quite a pleasant smile when I met her as that crowd went up to bed. Long may it last!"

"And Joey herself and Cecil have escaped, too," Kathy

Ferrars supplemented this. "I only wish Rosalie were stronger. She still looks awfully ill."

"She *has* been 'awfully ill', to quote you," Matron said. "However, it's only time and feeding up that are needed for her now. That temp took it out of her. I don't believe she has a rag she can wear with any decency! Her things just *flap* on her."

"We are going to have loud outcries about the way the girls have grown," Miss Annersley said, laughing. "Mdlle had everyone from the Fifths busy in needlework this afternoon, letting down hems to their fullest extent. And what Joey had to say about her twins when she first saw them was only beaten by Hilary's shrieks at her first glimpse of Marjory. All Felicity's frocks will have to be put aside for Cecil. They won't go near her now; and Joey had to hunt up some of the things Mike has outgrown for Felix."

"Well, at least it's ended now," Matron said with a sigh of relief.

Kathie Farrars echoed the sigh. "Thank goodness! I only hope we have no more awful trials for the rest of the term. I feel like something that's been put through the mangle a dozen times over!"

"Oh, so do I!" Miss Annersley assented.

Matron surveyed them both sharply. "You're tired out. Well, you can rest when half-term comes. Luckily, Easter's very early this year, so we can give a long half-term. As for you, Hilda Annersley, you are to go down to stay with Winifred Embury for the whole weekend, and she'll see you do nothing but rest. And now that we're really free from infection, we can get a temporary secretary to take the bulk of that work off your shoulders. Rosalie won't be fit for anything till next term, I'm afraid."

Matron got up. "It's late enough. Kathie, take yourself off to bed. Hilda, you can do the same thing. What's more, you can *stay* in it till I tell you to get up tomorrow. *You'll* be ill next, and we've had quite enough without that! Go on, both of you! I'm waiting!"

How the school would have chuckled if they could have seen not only Miss Ferrars, who was young enough not to count much, but the stately Head obeying Matron as meekly as the most junior girl of them all!

Chapter 8

HALF-TERM

MISS Dene was marched off to the south of France by her old friend, Evadne Lannis, who happened to be in Switzerland at the time. Evadne was the only child of an American millionaire. Expense meant nothing to her, and she insisted on bearing Rosalie Dene away to rest and recuperate in the best possible conditions.

Thursday saw the departure of nearly nine-tenths of the rest of the school to their homes or the homes of friends. In fact, when the Head had reckoned up the number of those for whom provision must be made, she found that there were only thirty-seven of them. Seven came from the two Sixths and Va and b accounted for eight more. The remainder were mainly younger girls.

Miss Burnett, the games mistress, instantly offered to take the entire twenty-two to Vevey where she had been proposing to sojourn herself. Her own special friend, Miss Armitage, who was responsible for all science below Vb, was going with her, so the Head had no scruples about accepting the offer.

None of Inter V had to be considered, and Mdlle offered to be responsible for the fifteen big girls. They were going to stay at a farmhouse not far from St. Moritz. Mdlle was an Alpiniste, an enthusiastic climber and outstandingly good at all winter sports. Kathy Ferrars, on hearing of their destination, eagerly begged leave to join them, and Nancy Wilmot, head of the maths, darkly hinted that no one was to be surprised if she turned up during the weekend. All the rest of the staff were off on a complete holiday—including the Head who was going to Lake Geneva where lived Mrs. Embury, very *nearly* an Old Girl, as she always vowed, and a firm friend of Miss Annersley's. Mrs. Embury had given all concerned her word of honour that the Head should spend the time in rest and recreation. Miss Wilson, her co-Head, would also be there, so Matron was hopeful that the weekend would prove a real holiday.

When the lists were put up, a good many people who were going home bewailed the fact that they must miss the Senior expedition.

"The Grisons!" Josette Russell exclaimed. "And I'm dying to go there! Oh, I do wish Mummy hadn't said I was to go home! How lucky some folk are!"

Lorraine Varley and Amandine Robinet, who had been expecting to go but, at the last moment, had been told they were going with Mr. and Mrs. Varley to Holland, agreed with her.

"Never mind; we'll tell you all about it when we meet again," Barbara Chester said soothingly. "Give me your address at the Hague—isn't that to be your headquarters?—and I might even rise to a picture postcard between you!"

They fell on her with cries of fury, but when Mr. Varley arrived to escort them to the Hague, they were ready for him. Both were very musical, and he had promised them two big concerts during the weekend.

Three other people were also deflected from the party, thanks to parents who had decided on the spur of the moment to come out to Switzerland and see for themselves that their daughters had taken no harm from the scarlet fever. So in the end, only ten girls were left to the tender mercies of Mdlle and Miss Ferrars. This party consisted of Mary-Lou and her "sister-by-marriage" as they called it, Verity Carey; Vi Lucy and Barbara Chester; Hilary Bennet and Prunella Davies and Naomi Elton, all from the two

Sixths; and three from Va, Monica Caird, Rosemary Lambe and Carol Younger who, despite a complete unlikeness of character, yet where bosom friends. Rosemary was an exceedingly pretty girl with hardly two ideas in her fluffy golden head; Monica was a sportswoman, pure and simple; Carol was a student, a girl who was never happier than when she had her teeth into a really stiff problem. What made these three so friendly was something that no one had ever been able to explain; but they were inseparables of the most marked type.

As there were so few of them they were to go by train from Chur. Dr. Graves, the owner of an outsize convertible had to go there on business connected with the Sanatorium, and he offered to take the entire party with him if they could crowd in.

The rest of the school had already departed when he drove up to be greeted with a resounding cheer from the twelve, who were waiting in the drive. Skis were strapped together and fixed to the roof, cases were piled up on the floor between the seats or under them and the excited girls packed in as best they could.

"This," the Head Girl remarked as she settled down in her seat, "is the goods! Are you all right, Hilary? It's more than a bit of a squash, isn't it?"

"I'm O.K.", Hilary said, laughing. "You all right, Barbara? Shove up a little, Carol. Vi has barely an inch to sit on."

"What a blessing none of us are fat!" Monica remarked as she, Rosemary and Carol all sat closer to give Vi a little more space. "Think what it would have been like with Hilda Jukes here!"

"In that case, someone—or two someones, even—would have had to ride on the roof on top of the skis," Barbara said with a chuckle.

Then they set off, along the Platz, to the head of the long, twisting road that ran direct to the plain from the shelf. Dr.

Graves put the car into bottom gear, jammed on his brakes and began to make the descent, slowly and cautiously.

Most of the girls paid no heed to it and went on chatting. But Mary-Lou, glancing across at Naomi, saw that her face was white as they negotiated the steep drop and bent across to speak to her.

"It's all right, Naomi," she said quietly. "I know the staff often go this way in the car, and I've done it myself once or twice. It's only a case of going slowly and carefully and having good brakes—and no one messes round with faulty brakes in this part of the world if they value their necks."

Naomi stiffened. "Oh, I'm not afraid," she said mendaciously. "I didn't expect anything quite so steep, though."

Prunella leapt into the breach. "I'm longing to see this farmhouse we're going to. Didn't Mrs. Maynard put us on to it? It'll be marvellous at that rate. And it will be fun, living with the people, won't it? By the way, does anyone know anything about St. Moritz? I like to know something about a place before I visit it."

"Apart from the fact that it's a world-famous spa and also a sports centre, I can't tell you a thing," Hilary said. "Thank goodness! Here we are at the end of that ghastly road!"

They had indeed reached the end of it, and now Dr. Graves swung out on to the magnificent autobahn, heading for the east past Interlaken and then on, along the south bank of Lake Brienz. Mary-Lou, still keeping watch on Naomi, saw the colour come back to her face, and was thankful.

Now there was nothing to prevent Dr. Graves from getting all he could out of the convertible, and the great motor-roads of Switzerland are kept in excellent fettle. They had set off early, and, in any case, this was not the height of the tourist season. They reached Chur in good time to have a meal there before they boarded the train to St. Moritz, which place they reached before darkness fell.

"This," said Mary-Lou with shocking disregard for school rules about the use of slang, "certainly is the job!"

They were standing outside the big farmhouse where Joey Maynard, who knew the owners very well, had arranged for them to stay during half term weekend. It was built of white stone with deeply pierced windows with oblique sides. Borders were painted down the edges of the walls, and between the windows were designs in gay colours that looked as fresh as if they had been done only the week before. The girls were startled when Herr Tratschin, the owner of the farm, assured them that the painting had been done in the previous spring and was due for renewal any time now. The big entrance door was finely arched at the top, and the arch bore another border to match those at the wall edges.

Miss Ferrars laughed. "Mary-Lou! And you are Head Girl! What appalling slang and what an example to the rest."

"Are we all here? No; I see Naomi isn't. And neither are Verity nor Barbara. What are they playing at? I thought we were to get off early so as to have plenty of time for exploring. Shall I go and hurry them up, Mdlle? Then we can get off," Hilary asked impatiently.

Mdlle nodded and she dashed back into the house, calling the three loiterers at the top of her voice. Verity appeared at once, full of apologies for being late.

"I've been talking to Frau Tratschin," she explained in her tiny, silvery voice.

Naomi came limping along after her; and Barbara was not far behind.

"And that's the last," Miss Ferrars said. "Get your skies on, all of you, and hurry up. I hope no one has forgotten her sticks?"

No one had. They hurriedly strapped on their skis, and then waited to hear what the next step was to be.

"We will visit the town first, I think," Mdlle said after a glance at her watch. "You will enjoy the shops and the lake—we are a little far from the lake here. Also, there is plenty to see that will interest you. Naomi, we have a toboggan for you, as we must not let you tire yourself. Who will tow Naomi?" She turned to the others while Naomi's lips went down in the familiar droop. She hated to have any notice drawn to her disabilities.

"I will!" Even Rosemary joined in the chorus, and Naomi suddenly flushed. She knew well enough that she was a favourite with no one. She had given none of them a chance to know her or like her. And yet, though she would never have owned it, the steady kindliness and consideration shown her by almost everyone was beginning to take effect on her.

"Prunella and Hilary to begin with, I think," Mdlle said after a moment. "It's not very far—about a couple of kilometres. Once we reach it, we will leave toboggan and skies at a shop on the outskirts where I am known and then we can all walk. Two others will draw Naomi home when we have had enough," she added with a trill of laughter. "See, Naomi! Here comes your carriage!"

A small boy appeared round the corner of the house, pulling after him a toboggan. Mdlle smiled at him, said, "Danke, Gaudenz!" and handed him a slab of chocolate in exchange for the ropes. He gave her a shy grin and an even shyer, "Danke, gnädige Fräulein!" before he went scampering back.

Meanwhile, the girls had crowded round the little toboggan, exclaiming in delight at its beauty. It was of wood and the sides and up-curving back were adorned with a delightful design of alpine flora with a perfectly carved chamois surmounting the top of the back. It was well-cushioned, too, and Vi expressed the feeling of everyone when she cried, "Oh, what a marvellous thing!"

Mdlle laughed. "Sit down, Naomi, and let us pack you in. That is right! And here is a rug in case you feel cold with sitting."

Hilary and Prunella took up the ropes, once Naomi was settled, and they sped off over the frozen snow which, today, was glittering under the bright sun in a way that made them thankful for their coloured glasses.

"We can have time to look round properly, can't we?" Barbara Chester asked coaxingly. Then, in tones of surprise, "Why! Isn't that the church spire over there? But it's *leaning*!"

"Yes," Mdlle told her tranquilly. "The leaning spire of St. Moritz is well known. And yes, Barbara; you may have plenty of time to see all there is to see. But not too much. Snow is forecast for later in the day, and I should prefer to have you all safely in the house before it comes. So do not loiter. And now, here is my shop. Stop, all, and unstrap your skies. Naomi, Miss Ferrars and I will help you to your feet. Wait a moment, ma petite! There! That is right!"

Vi had pulled off her skis and handed them to Mary-Lou. Now she came forward, crooking an elbow invitingly. "Will you have an arm, Madame? Pray do me the honour."

Naomi glanced up at her enchanting face and saw it alive with laughter. Something melted within her, and her own rare laughter answered as she slipped a hand through the arm, saying, "Thank you. I shall certainly feel safer."

The others hurriedly collected their skis and sticks and followed Mdlle to the shop where she addressed a few words to the girl in charge. Everything was handed over, and then they all set out in a body, chattering hard, to explore the little town.

They wandered around until it was nearly time for Mittagessen and Naomi was beginning to look very tired. She had walked more that morning than she had done for some years past. Mdlle had kept an eye on her and she decided that it was enough for one morning. Naomi could spend the afternoon lying down if she felt like it. And so might Verity Carey, who was also looking as if she had done enough. The rest were full of vim still, and cried out when the mistress told them that they must return. However, Mdlle, though she might slacken the reins considerably when she saw fit, always knew when to pull them in. They set off back to the shop where they retrieved their skis and the toboggan, and

71

then, with Mary-Lou and Vi on the ropes and Verity between Monica and Hilary, they all whirled back to the farmhouse.

"I'm very much afraid we shall have snow," Verity said as they went. "The sun's vanished and those clouds look awfully heavy, Mdlle. Shall we get back before it comes, do you think?"

"But yes; certainly." Mdlle said. "I have been watching the sky, and I know we can manage it."

All the same, she gave the order to quicken pace, and they flew across the snow which now had lost all its glitter. Frau Tratschin was at the door, watching for them. When they came skimming up, she gave an exclamation of relief.

"I am glad to see you all safely here! The sky means mischief, beyond a doubt. Come in—come in, all! Mittagessen is ready and the soup is hot. Hasten, now. Ah! Here it comes!"

The last girl passed in, and she shut the door with a bang on the whirling snow that had just begun to fall with a force that showed it meant to keep on and there would be no further expeditions that day.

Chapter 9

MARY-LOU TAKES A CHANCE

"WHAT shall we do with ourselves?" Verity asked as they helped to clear the table after Mittagessen.

"Oh, we'll manage to amuse ourselves all right," her "sister-by-marriage" replied before she went off to the kitchen with a loaded tray. She was back a few minutes later, her hands equally full, but this time with a zither.

"Where on earth did you get that?" Miss Ferrars demanded.

"From Frau Tratschin. I saw it hanging on the wall when I took the tray out, and I asked her if she played it. She said it was her son's. Then she asked if any of us played it, and if we'd like to have it to amuse us. I told her I hadn't an idea about the playing, but I thought we'd rather love to borrow it. So she handed it over. *Does* anyone know how the thing works? What about you, Naomi?" She had seen a strange look on Naomi's face, and she knew that the girl loved music.

Naomi shook her head. "I've heard it played, of course; but I've never attempted to touch one. I couldn't do a thing with it."

"I can play a little," Mdlle said, with an amused smile. "I think, though, that you will enjoy yourselves more if you try to pick out tunes for yourselves. Did Frau Tratschin give you the plectron, Mary-Lou? For, if not, I fear you may have sore fingers if you try it. Some of the strings are of wire of various kinds."

Mary-Lou felt in the breast pocket of her blazer and

73

produced a small ring which, as Mdlle explained, you wore on the thumb of your right hand. A tiny quill attached, plucked the strings.

"How do you hold it?" Vi asked curiously.

"You place it on the table—so." Mdlle took the instrument from Mary-Lou, sat down at the table, and showed them the correct position. "The air is played with the thumb and the bass accompaniment is played with the other fingers of the right hand. The strings are divided into groups of five notes. To make others, you stop the strings with the fingers of the left hand. Keep the right wrist on the side of the zither parallel with these pins which are known as hitch pins, and the thumb over the finger-board."

As she talked, she plucked the strings, first softly and then with considerable force, and the girls all exclaimed at the sweetness of the notes.

"Yes; it is a very good zither. A large one, also, as it has forty-two strings. Now I shall leave you to amuse yourselves. I have letters to write and shall go to my room. Miss Ferrars, what will you do?"

Kathy Ferrars bounced off the stool on which she had been sitting. "I've letters to write myself. I owe at least three. After that, I shall indulge in a new novel I brought with me and be thoroughly lazy." She paused and glanced at Mdlle. She remembered that that lady had said Naomi ought to lie down that afternoon.

Mdlle took no notice. She had seen the colour come back to the girl's face after a delicious meal. Naomi was laughing and talking—not much, it is true, but more than she had ever done before. Not for worlds would Mdlle have put a stop to this approach to normal girlhood. She merely smiled at the girls, remarking that if they wanted her, they knew where to find her, and went off with her colleague.

Left alone, the girls began to experiment with the zither. It was not easy, and one by one they gave it up, even Vi, who, as a violinist, managed better than most. Verity, who had stayed in the background, came forward now.

"Let me try," she pleaded. "I'd like to try to make tunes on it. What a lovely rich sound it has!"

Mary-Lou pushed it across the table to her, pulling off the plectron with which she had been producing some odd sounds, and putting it into her hand. "There you are! Go ahead and see what you can make of it. It's plain that music is *not* my strong point. You go on with it, Verity."

Verity fitted on the plectron and touched a string. "I think I can see how to manage. Are you all quite sure you won't mind if I play round with it a little?"

No one made any objection. Verity carried her treasure off to one of the windows, where it fitted nicely on the broad sill, and proceeded to enjoy herself. The rest, chattering gaily, paid little heed to her. After years of boarding school they were quite able to shut their ears to any extraneous sounds. Only Naomi frowned as the zither player made false notes and harmonies now and then.

Mary-Lou glancing up on one of these occasions, saw it and guessed that Verity's stumbling efforts were setting her teeth on edge. She lifted her voice.

"Hi, Verity! Can't you take that thing off somewhere where we don't have to listen to you killing pigs or whatnot?"

Verity remained calm under this cheerful insult. "I want to ask Frau Tratschin about one or two things. I'll take it to the kitchen."

She picked it up and vanished into the kitchen, where Frau Tratschin, her domestic labours over for the moment, was sitting at her lace-pillow, making the bobbins fly as she twisted her threads, moved her pins and produced a cobwebby effect that made the would-be musician exclaim in delighted amazement before she settled down to her questions. The kindly farmer's wife was pleased to give any help she could, and Verity and she were soon going ahead.

Meanwhile, most of the others were seated round the

table, playing an exciting game of rummy. Mary-Lou had retired to a window-seat with a book, and Naomi was at the other with another book.

Presently the new girl glanced across at the tall prefect absorbed in her reading. She forgot her own, and stayed gazing at Mary-Lou with a very thoughtful expression on her face. Presently that young woman felt the gaze, and looked up with a smile. Something she saw in the other girl's eyes made her close the book, get up and come over to her.

"Bored, are you? What have you got there?" She glanced at the book. "Goodness, Naomi! I don't know if we're supposed to read that."

Naomi looked down at *Humphrey Clinker*. "Why not? Not that I'm exactly enamoured of it. What have you got?"

"A thriller. I rather love a really good whodunnit, don't you?"

"I can't say. I don't think I've ever read one. I say, Mary-Lou, could we go upstairs to a bedroom, do you think? I—I'd like to talk to you."

"O.K., where's your stick? Those rowdies," Mary-Lou cast a grin in the direction of the card-players whose shrieks certainly merited her epithet, "will never miss us. We'll go and have a good natter together."

However, when they were finally settled in the bedroom Naomi was sharing with three of the others, she speedily found that she had let herself in for a good deal more than she had bargained for.

The Head Girl insisted on Naomi lying down on her bed and being tucked up under a big rug, while she herself calmly robbed Prunella Davies's bed of another before sitting down on a chair close at hand. Naomi gave her another of those queerly thoughtful looks. Her back had been aching and it was bliss to lie down like this. But how did Mary-Lou know it? She had said nothing.

"How did you know?" she asked abruptly.

"Know what?" Mary-Lou demanded.

"Know about my back."

"Well, I thought you looked all in, and I know what it is to have an aching back," Mary-Lou explained. She paused and fished in her pockets, finally coming up with a slab of chocolate. "Have some choc? We may as well be comfy."

"How do you mean?" Naomi persisted as she accepted the chocolate.

"In what way? Oh, about the back! Well, you see, two years or so ago I was mixed up in a toogganing accident and dished my own back pretty badly. Oh, it's all right now, thank goodness; only aches when I'm really deadly tired. But for quite a time it was weak. In fact, if you really want to know, there *were* two or three days when no one knew whether I would ever walk again."

"How simply awful!" Naomi spoke with a fervour that sprang from her own experience. "How did it happen?"

"I told you—a toboggan accident. I bashed my head—I had a lump like a football on the back—and bruised my spine. That's when my hair was cut. It had been as straight as a yardstick before then. But they had to shave my head, and when my hair grew again, it grew *curls*! So, on the whole," Mary-Lou concluded with some complacency, "I reckoned I'd gained by it."

"Well, I didn't gain a thing by *my* accident," Naomi told her bitterly. "I only lost. Before it happened I was as straight as anyone. I was keen on dancing, and my people promised me I should have my chance to train as a ballet dancer."

Like a flash Mary-Lou's warm hand caught one of hers. "Oh, I'm so very sorry!" she cried. "That must have been dreadful for you!"

"Dreadful? You can't begin to know how dreadful. Because my parents died in the same fire. I lost my father and mother and my power to dance all at once. Do you wonder," Naomi wound up, still in that bitter tone, "that I don't believe in God? Or if He really is there, then He just doesn't care."

77

Mary-Lou remained very still for a minute or two. Somehow she felt that if she could only think of the right things to say and do, she might be able to put an end to this unhealthy way of thinking. How could anyone bearing the disabilities she did go through life without some help, and who could give it but God?

"Naomi, I didn't understand. But oh, don't either say or think such dreadful things. They simply aren't true."

"How do you know? *You* have got better. You can walk and run and dance as well as ever. I'm done for anything of that kind. I've been all over to all sorts of wonderful surgeons. They all say the same thing. The ligaments or something are shrivelled, and it's caused the shape I am now."

"Well, I don't know enough about that to argue with you; but the minute I can get hold of him I'm going to talk to Uncle Jack," Mary-Lou said firmly.

"Who is he?" Naomi asked languidly. She was tired physically by her morning's activities, and the sudden letting down of the barriers even by so little, had wearied her mentally.

"He's Dr. Maynard—Aunt Joey's husband. He's head of the San at the Platz, you know. He's brilliant, I've heard people say. And what's more, he manages to keep abreast of all the latest cures. Naomi, don't give up hope! They can do such marvellous things now with surgery, and every day, almost, they make new discoveries. Oh, I don't say you would be able to dance—"

"I couldn't anyhow. I'm too old to start now," Naomi said. "But never mind that. I've had all these years to make up my mind to it that that is *off*. But if it was possible for me to be straight again and walk about and move normally, oh, Mary-Lou, if it ever happened, I'd believe in God again and love Him!" Then her excitement died as suddenly as it had come, and she added wearily, "But I don't see how it could happen. It's just your thinking of it."

"But you could *hope* about it, couldn't you?" Mary-Lou pleaded. "And another thing, Naomi, why do you go round as if—as if you always had your arm up to protect your head against having your ears boxed? I mean that metaphorically, of course. You must have been with some really unpleasant people if you can imagine that's the sort of thing you'll get from us."

Naomi flushed. "I hate being pitied and looked at as if I were something out of a wild beast show! I loathe it when people *stare* at me and look sorry for me!"

"Oh, don't be so silly! No one is likely to do that to you if you'll only behave naturally. People," said Mary-Lou wisely, "are awfully given to taking you as you think of yourself. Of course, if that's your idea of yourself, you can't very well expect them to think differently."

Naomi's jaw dropped. Never had anyone talked to her like this before. She remained silent, and Mary-Lou, having said as much as she dared at one time, was silent, too. She glanced at the girl on the bed rather fearfully. Naomi was lying quite still and her eyes were closed. She got up to her feet cautiously, but at her movement, the eyes opened.

"I'm not asleep," Naomi said, "or not yet. All the same, I'd like to be alone for a while now. You've given me something to think about."

"O.K. I'll go down, then, and join the rummy gang," Mary-Lou agreed affably. "You do rather look as if a nap would do you good." As she turned to go, a hand came out from under the rugs and caught her wrist.

"I'll think it over. And Mary-Lou! I know you do truly believe in God and all that. But you haven't had to face what I have. Only," she added, "if there *should* ever be anything in what you said about modern surgery, and it really happens, then I *will* believe. I couldn't do anything else!"

"Right! That's a bargain!" Mary-Lou assented. "Now I'm going and you try to get a sleep. You'll feel a lot better after it."

And she left the room and raced off downstairs to join the rummy players. But she had certainly started something that afternoon, though neither she nor Naomi could possibly know how it would all end.

Chapter 10

AVALANCHE!

NEXT morning they woke up to find that the snow had died off during the night, and the day was sunny and still. Mdlle ordained that they should skate today. Naomi could not skate, of course, but a small high-backed sledge was procured. She was packed in, and the girls took it in turns to push her round the lake. When they finally left off to go and seek a sheltered nook where they could devour their sandwiches, cakes and hot coffee with which Frau Tratschin, warned beforehand by Mdlle, had provided them, everyone was flushed and laughing and eager to go at it again as soon as possible.

They had to leave the lake when the sun set, but Mdlle informed them that, as it was full moon, they should go for a moonlight ski after Abendessen. This was something quite new, and they enjoyed themselves enormously though they were all tired when they finally returned to the farm, where hot milk and buns awaited them before they went off to bed where even Naomi fell asleep as soon as her head touched the pillow.

The next day was Sunday, which meant church for all of them. Mdlle took the Catholic girls to High Mass, and Miss Ferrars went off with the rest to the Lutheran church since there was no English service for them to attend that day.

"Wish we'd gone with you," Mary-Lou grumbled later to Hilary. "I don't like the Lutheran service, and it was all in German, of course, and a fearfully long sermon into the bargain. I found it frightfully difficult to follow, and, to crown everything, I think the pastor must have either just *got* false teeth or else was trying out a new set that didn't really fit."

However, Mddle took them off on a good ski-run in the afternoon, so she forgot her discontent and in the evening, as the weather still continued fine, they went for a short run between Kaffee and Kuchen and Abendessen. Bedtime came early. As Mdlle pointed out, they had had a strenuous time, and on the morrow they were to go into the mountains for tobogganing.

Monday was a grey day and unseasonably warm. Mdlle looked uneasily at the sky, but the clouds were fairly high so she agreed to the tobogganing, though Herr Tratschin warned the girls not to shout too much when they were in the mountains.

"But why not?" Mary-Lou demanded.

"Because, meine Fräulein, it may be that with this fresh snow and then the warmer weather some of the cornices are loose and ready to fall—though I am sure it is safe where I am sending you," he added.

"Do you think he's said anything about it to Mdlle?" Hilary asked when he had gone.

"Oh, sure to. We're going where he advises. He wouldn't send us into danger, you know!" Mary-Lou sounded very certain.

"No; I suppose not. O.K. How do we divide up?" Hilary asked.

Mary-Lou eyed her warily. "I'm going to ask you people to let Naomi come with us if you don't mind. I've had a word with Verity, and she says she doesn't mind going with some of the others. You see, she's so helpless in some ways—Naomi, I mean—and I'd like to be sure she was with people who understand. You don't mind, do you?"

"I can think of other folk I'd rather have with us," Hilary said drily. "Still, I see your point."

At this point, Miss Ferrars arrived with Naomi, so the talk stopped. Mary-Lou gave her invitation, and Verity joined up with Barbara, Prunella and Vi, while the three inseperables made a dive for the first toboggan without any argument. The last toboggan was taken by the two mistresses. Finally, they all set off, Naomi travelling as usual on her toboggan.

They all went on skis. Herr Tratschin had told them there was a hut at the foot of the slope where they could leave all their gear, including their midday meal, for Mdlle had said they would spend the day tobogganing. This was their last full day, for though they were returning by train, they must leave shortly after midday in order to reach the school before Abendessen.

They went flying over the snow, laughing and talking as they went, and presently they were beginning to go up until at last they reached the small hut Herr Tratschin had mentioned. Beyond, the slope rose sharply for some distance before going in a gentle curve round the side.

"This is something like!" Mary-Lou proclaimed in her usual clarion tones.

"Hi! If you go on yelling like that, you'll bring the entire lot down on us!" Hilary cried, laughing.

Mary-Lou laughed. "Sorry! I didn't mean to yell. But it really is something! Our own isn't bad, but this must be four times the distance. What a gorgeous run down we shall have! Mdlle, how far up may we go?"

"I will come with you and show you," Mdlle replied.

"And Mary-Lou, do remember what Hilary says. Herr Tratschin assures me it is safe enough here; but you would not wish to involve us all in an avalanche?"

"I would not." Mary-Lou's voice had dropped. "I'll remember, Mdlle."

Mdlle started them off, warning each girl as she passed to remember not to shout, and presently the long steep slope was dotted with figures. Mary-Lou and Hilary led, still pulling Naomi on their toboggan. Vi and Co. followed, with

Verity as passenger. She was not very strong and apt to tire quickly. Monica, Carol and Rosemary came next, and the two mistresses last of all.

The road led up the straight slope, round a spur of the mountain, and on up to a shelf where stood another hut. They had it to themselves, and there was a silence up here that overawed even Mary-Lou the exuberant.

"The hut seems to be closed," she murmured softly to Mdlle. "Do you know what it is?"

"Me, I had no idea of it," she said. She wrinkled her brows thoughtfully. "No; I am sure—very sure—that Herr Tratschin never spoke of a second hut."

"Perhaps he forgot about it," Mary-Lou suggested. "It might be a herdsman's hut for the summer months when the cows are up, but closed during the winter, and so he never thought of it again."

"Yes; that might be," Mdlle agreed. She glanced round at the mountain slopes towering above them, white with their thick covering of snow. "Well, we must ask him when we return. Meantime, let us toboggan. And remember, all; no screaming! I see no cornice very near nor overhanging this part, but we have had new snow, and today is certainly warm. Who goes first?"

That set them off, and presently the four toboggans were flying down the long incline at ever-increasing speed. By the time they had done the run four or five times, everyone was glowing and flushed. Even Naomi had forgotten her woes and grievances. She was laughing softly and her eyes were shining with genuine pleasure. Mdlle saw it and nudged her colleague to draw her attention to it. *This* was not the Naomi they had all known so far.

By the time a halt was called for Mittagessen the sun was blazing down, so that more than one of the girls begged permission to discard some part of her clothing. It was forbidden, of course. No one wanted them to wind up the holiday with odd cases of pneumonia, and if the sun was hot at present, there was no saying how long he would continue.

They went to the lower hut to reclaim their knapsacks, and then moved away to a little grove of birches behind it, where they all squatted down on the toboggans, and enjoyed the delicious lunch Frau Tratschin had packed for them. But once their meal was over, they were all anxious to resume their tobogganing. Mdlle gave the word, and once more they climbed up the long slopes to the closed hut, where they stood talking in undertones and laughing softly.

Suddenly, without warning, the great stillness was filled with a terrible roaring which grew and grew until it seemed there was nothing left in the world but the thunderous noise. The blue sky overhead vanished. A cornice of fresh snow overhanging the straight part of the run had become loosened from its hold by the heat of the sun and came crashing down, tearing away from the mountain slopes great rocks and boulders, tree trunks and slabs of earth as it fell.

The girls screamed and made for the shelter of the hut. Mary-Lou beat on the door with fists and feet until the latch gave way beneath her assault, and they all practically fell into the place.

All? No; Naomi, lifted off her feet by the frantic rush of the others, fell headlong just outside. Mary-Lou, who had managed to keep her balance, saw her, even as Mdlle struggled madly to her own feet. Instantly, the prefect dashed out again, regardless of the rain of pebbles, earth and snow that was showering down, grasped the other girl under the arms, and dragged her into the hut in one lightning-like movement. Then the rest of the avalanche came down and the light was blotted out completely. When all was still again, they found that their route down was blocked by a huge mass of snow, rubble and pine trunks, though the hut, built under a bulge in the mountain-wall had escaped. Most of them were bruised and cut from the flying débris; and on the floor lay Naomi, still, white and senseless—to all appearance, dead.

Chapter 11

IN THE HUT

"MARY-LOU—are you awake?"

Mary-Lou, dozing fitfully on the floor of the herdsmen's hut, roused up, rolled over and stretched out a hand. Naomi, who had spoken, clutched it in a feverish grip. She had come round shortly before Mdlle had ordained that they must all lie down and try to sleep. She was very white, and there was a nasty gash from her ear to her chin, but that was swiftly remedied. Matron never allowed anyone to go off on an expedition without a first-aid kit, and Mdlle and Miss Ferrars had both been carrying theirs strapped to their backs when the disaster happened.

Most of the girls were too worn out by the time the moon rose, flooding into the hut doorway, which they had to leave open as a boulder, protruding into the one room, prevented them from shutting it, to be anything but sleepy. They had soon dropped off, much to the relief of the two mistresses. Only Mary-Lou, who had strained her back slightly in that wild effort to save Naomi, and Naomi herself whose shocked nerves would allow her no chance to rest, were awake now.

"You're all right, Naomi. We're safe enough here. Can't you sleep? Let's see if I can make you more comfy." Mary-Lou slipped an arm under the thin shoulders, raising Naomi a little and the younger girl suddenly clung to her.

"Mary-Lou, aren't you—afraid?"

Mary-Lou considered. "I can't say I'm exactly pleased with this set-up. Who would be? I'm frantically hungry, and

86

goodness only knows when we shall get out of this. But as for afraid; no, I'm not exactly afraid."

"I am," Naomi said simply. "I'm *terribly* afraid."

"But why? They'll get to us in time—and not such a long time at that, either."

"How can you possibly know that?" Naomi demanded.

"Well, use your common sense! The Tratschins know exactly where we are. You can bet that when we never turned up by Abendessen, even if they hadn't heard of the avalanche before, they'd simply raise the neighbourhood to get at us. 'Tisn't as if we'd gone off into the blue and no one knew *where* to look for us, you know."

"I hadn't thought that out," Naomi confessed. "Yes; I think you're right there."

"I know I am," Mary-Lou said with a calm certainty that made Naomi gasp. "They'll get us out one way or another. But in the meantime, unless the herdsmen left a few tins or something up here, we're going to have to go on frightfully short rations for the time being. And I *am* very worried about what our own folk are going through. I should think they'll go frantic if we aren't yanked out pretty quickly."

"I never thought of their side of it," Naomi said. Then she shivered.

"Cold?" Mary-Lou asked. "Sorry I can't do any more about it. Get as close to me as you can and we'll keep each other warm."

"No; I'm not really cold. But I was thinking—oh, Mary-Lou! You know how—how I've thought and talked about things. Do—do you think God's punishing me this way?"

"Talk sense!" said Mary-Lou. "Honestly, Naomi, you simply *can't* talk rot like that! That would be punishing the rest of us as well, and that would be unfair. God's never unfair, let me tell you. Pull yourself together and for goodness sake stop talking such rot!"

"Are you sure?" Naomi cried. "Oh, Mary-Lou, are you quite *sure*?"

"'Sh! You'll wake the rest if you yell like that! Of course I'm sure—positive."

"And you do truly think that they'll get us out sooner or later?"

"Certainly they will! What *were* you imagining?" Mary-Lou gave a low chuckle. "Honestly, Naomi! You pipe down and try to go to sleep, and so will I. Stop thinking, anyhow, for your thoughts are simply crackers."

Naomi sighed and fell silent. Soon Mary-Lou went under a deep wave of sleep and Naomi lay quietly, turning over in her mind what the Head Girl had said to her during that eventful weekend, but she drowsed off finally. It was broad daylight before there was any further sound from the hut, barring the quiet breathing of the sleepers and an occasional mutter from Barbara, who was given to talking in her sleep. A ray of morning sunlight found its way through the space above the boulder and struck full across the eyes of Kathy Ferrars, who was lying against the opposite wall. She stirred sleepily, wondering what had become of the bedclothes. Then she opened her eyes, stared round wildly, and came to full consciousness.

Afterwards, Kathy said that she had never imagined herself in such a scene. The girls were lying closely huddled together on the floor. A hump near the boulder represented Mdlle, who had insisted on taking the outside place. Everyone was sleeping as if for a wager. She decided to make a start towards some sort of a meal. She herself was famishing, and she could guess what the girls would be like when they woke up.

Her first step was to collect her knapsack. She had retained it the day before because in it was their first-aid kit, but she knew that it also held a slab of chocolate and at least one orange. It was not much for twelve people, but it was better than nothing. First came the kit. Then the chocolate, two oranges, a bag which held a bun and another with three sandwiches which were dry and curling at the edges, but still edible.

"Well, that's a lot better than I expected," she muttered. "Some of the girls are safe to have oddments of chocolate, too. What's this—oh, glory! Biscuits! I forgot I'd shoved that packet in at the last moment. Wonder what Jeanne has?"

As if she had heard her own name, Mdlle stirred and then awoke. She sat up, stretching herself, and Kathy clambered across the legs of the girls, and reached her side with her treasure.

"Jeanne! Do you think I could possibly get up that rock and bring some snow in? Then, if we can only find something to burn, I've chocolate here, and we could melt the snow and give the girls a hot drink. And I've a few fragments of food as well. What have you got?"

Mdlle felt in her pockets and produced another slab of chocolate and two packets of almonds and raisins, which set her colleague to searching her own pockets from which she produced a third packet as well as her cigarette case and lighter.

"It'll be what you might call a mixed meal," she said with a low laugh, "but better than nothing. I suppose the men aren't likely to have left any tins of anything. Where should we look?"

Mdlle stood up and looked round. Her eye was caught by a kind of corner shelf in the far corner. "But I think over there would be the most likely place."

"It would be! I suppose the girls *have* only two legs each, but when I was coming to you just now, I wondered if some of them had developed an extra one overnight."

At this point Hilary suddenly sat up yawning. She looked round. "Lumme! Where have I got to?" she demanded loudly.

It acted like the rising bell at school. One by one the girls woke up and gave tongue. Finally Mary-Lou staggered to her feet, and gazed round on them.

"*Well!*" she observed in shocked tones. "A more ghastly collection of scarecrows I never beheld in my life!"

"You're none so beautiful yourself!" Vi retorted. "Your face is filthy and you've straws in your hair!"

"I'd like a wash," Verity remarked plaintively. "And I'd like a drink and something to eat! Oh, and I've got something to eat! I've just remembered! I've got a packet of figs in one of my pockets."

This set them all off. By the time the pockets were emptied a miscellaneous heap of chocolate, almonds and raisins, biscuits, figs and dates were in the middle of the floor. Then Miss Ferrars, who had been investigating, let out a veritable yell of triumph and emerged from the corner with a flat cake of stale black bread in either hand.

"There's something more there," Miss Ferrars cried, going back to rummage. She produced two more of the rocklike cakes and two tins of condensed milk.

"Oh, well, we shan't starve for the present, anyhow!" Monica said.

Verity had come to the boulder and was gazing up at it. "I'm the smallest of us. If some of you folk would give me a leg up, I believe I could crawl through that space and get some snow. If we buried the bread in it, it would soften by degrees, and then we could eat it."

"We'll do better than that," Mdlle said in her own tongue. She had been rummaging on her own account, and had discovered a faggot of resinous twigs and branches. "If we can find a can or a pan, we will build a fire. Miss Ferrars has her lighter, and we can mix the chocolate with snow, and that will give us a hot drink. Look round, all of you, and see if you can find something."

It was Naomi who spied, tucked up among the rafters, a large flat pan. Hilary made "a back", and Mary-Lou climbed up and managed to bring the pan down. Meanwhile, on the flat stones which clearly served the men for a hearth, Mdlle piled up twigs and branches, the lighter was put to work, and in three minutes a fine cloud of smoke poured out into the room, setting them all coughing and choking as the twigs caught and blazed up.

This lasted only a minute or so. There was a hole in the roof, and presently the smoke was pouring up through it. They had their fire!

The next thing was to get the snow. Mdlle was doubtful about letting Verity or anyone else venture out, but Verity insisted. She easily wriggled through the space, and presently she was looking through into the hut.

"It's all right, Mdlle. There's a kind of shelf in the rock here and I can stoop down and scoop up the snow, if you'll give me something to do it with."

This was a puzzle. The herdsmen had left no mugs or cans. Finally, Miss Ferrars turned out all the oddments from the first-aid box, and that was passed through the opening to Verity, who set to work at once.

It was a long slow job. The pan had been placed before the fire which was now dying down to a bed of glowing ash and wood, and they ran to and fro with the piled-up box and emptied it as quickly as they could. Verity's long curls lost the ribbon which kept them back from her face. She was scarlet, and before long her back was aching badly; but she stuck to it despite Mdlle's commands to give it up and come back.

"Oh, I must get some more, Mdlle. I'm sure there isn't enough to give us even half a cup each. When it melts it always goes less. And then it isn't even as if it were just snow. There's such a lot of mud and stuff mixed with it."

This was all true, but would have mattered nothing to Mdlle if she had only been in a position to enforce the order Verity so calmly and stubbornly refused to obey. She was a quiet, gentle girl as a rule, but, as everyone knew, she had a marked streak of obstinacy in her which, when touched, was apt to overlay her other qualities.

Mary-Lou put her oar in. "Verity Anne Carey! You do as you're told and come back at once! You're worrying everyone, and it's jolly unfair of you!"

Verity's face appeared in the gap. "How full is that pan thing?" she demanded.

"Er—well, quite full enough to give us each a little. You come back—*What's that*?" She broke off sharply, and Verity wriggled round to stare down into the valley.

The sound which had startled the pair of them was a long yodel. It was repeated, and then Verity gave vent to a positive howl.

"There are people down there! They've come to find us! Give me something to wave, someone—quick!"

"You be careful!" Mary-Lou warned her as she stripped off her scarf and pushed it through. "For mercy's sake don't fall off that perch of yours!"

"O.K. I'll be careful," Verity promised. She turned carefully so that she was facing down the slope. She could just glimpse the valley and the people looking like ants far below, but she could hear clearly the yodelling which was going on continually now as one person after another took it up.

Everyone in the hut could hear it now, and they left the fire and the pan where the snow was melting fast, and crowded round the foot of the rock at their side.

"Let's yodel back," Hilary cried. "If we all do it together, they'll hear us."

"Good idea!" Miss Ferrars exclaimed. "Take your time from me! One—two—three—*yodel*!"

The noise they made was enough to waken the dead. Verity, acting as look-out, reported results excitedly, clinging to her shelf with fingers and toes.

"They're moving about—they've heard—I don't think they can see us, but someone is waving something! They're coming—oh, I can't see now! But I'm *sure* they're coming to find us and rescue us! Shall I come in now? I can't help any more."

"But yes, my child; certainly come in, and at once!" Mdlle said firmly. "Stand back, girls! Be careful, Verity!"

Mary-Lou scrambled up the far side of the boulder and

thrust out her head to watch the progress of her "sister-by-marriage". It was not easy. The Head Girl watched her slow movements with fear and trembling. A great mass of soft snow mixed with rubble and earth was piled up just below, and if Verity fell, she ran a grave risk of being buried alive. She did slip once, and Mary Lou, making a mighty effort, got an arm through just in time to grip her wrist and save her from going altogether. To the two who knew what had happened, it seemed an eternity before Verity found her footing, though it was a bare twenty seconds. Then she was safe again, and a moment or two later she crawled through the narrow opening and descended headfirst on top of Monica, Hilary and Prunella, who were standing by ready to catch her.

Mdlle took tiny Verity in her arms. "Are you hurt, chérie?"

"No—except that Mary-Lou nearly wrenched my arm out of its socket when she grabbed me just now. But if she hadn't . . ." Verity shuddered.

"Forget it!" Miss Ferrars said quickly. "Two of you girls get that pan on the fire and bring it to the boil. The snow's pretty well melted now. Vi, sort out the chocolate and break it up. We'll have to drink out of my box and that means putting the chocolate into it and pouring the water in on top. Where are those barley sugars Naomi handed out? Here, Verity! Suck this. Anyone got a knife? You, Hilary? Then pierce holes in this tin of condensed milk."

Thanks to her wit, they were all soon at work, and Verity, who had been lowered to the hay, was recovering the colour which had left her face.

"My legs feel all gone," she complained. "And oh, how my back aches with stooping. I've never been half sorry enough for you, Mary-Lou—or you, Naomi. I shall know how to sympathise now when either of you has backache!"

"The pan's beginning to bubble," Vi said. "Get your scarves off, everyone. The rim will be blazing hot."

"Here, let me! I can lift it!" big Monica said imperiously, taking the scarves. She lifted the pan carefully, and set it down on the floor. "Now how do we manage?"

"Build up the fire first!" Barbara cried, bringing an armful of twigs and branches. "If they see the smoke, they can find us quicker."

"Good, Barbara!" Mdlle exclaimed. "As for how we are to manage, we must take out a boxful at a time, break up the chocolate into it and add the milk. We cannot pour from that big pan or we shall spill most of it. Do not fill the box, though. Miss Ferrars, will you take charge, please? Give Verity hers first."

Kathy Ferrars dipped the box in by its lid, skimming the top of the water to leave the mud behind as far as possible. Chocolate was broken into it, and then the condensed milk was added. It was very thick and poured slowly, but at last, each girl and both mistresses had had a hot drink of sorts. Then the food was shared out, and, once that had been eaten, there was no more to do but to sit and wait.

A long wait it was, too. It was halfway through the afternoon before the prisoners were relieved by Herr Tratschin's voice sounding through the smoke-vent in the roof.

"Hé, there! Is all well?"

Mdlle had been standing by the boulder, listening anxiously. Now she ran across the floor like one of the girls. "Herr Tratschin? Yes; we are all safe. Can you get us out soon?"

"We dare not try to free the doorway, for what has fallen is soft and lies deep—very deep. We must clear the roof and reach you that way. And to do that, men must be let down by rope. But have no fear. Soon we will have you out. First, though, put the fire out."

Greatly wondering what he meant, Mdlle summoned Miss Ferrars, and together they carefully raked out the embers of the fire. The girls stood waiting to trample out each little heap as it fell to the ground, and Hilary, by a sudden

94

inspiration, poured the mud from the pan over everything when the hearthstone was bare.

Mdlle nodded approval as she stopped up to the vent and called, "It is done."

"Good—that is very good! Now I lower a parcel of food and another of coffee in flasks, very hot and strong. Watch for him!"

Two great bundles came slowly through and Mdlle caught first one and then the other, unfastened them and handed them over to her colleague.

"Now," ordered Herr Tratschin, "all go to the far side and stay there, for we come to pull the logs from the roof, and there are rocks tied on which may fall."

They all skipped across to the farther side as fast as they could, and then, while the two mistresses handed out coffee and great rolls sliced and filled with butter and meat, they heard the men beginning to work on the roof.

"This *is* an adventure!" Vi said as she finished her first roll and held out her hand for a second. "But I do hope the family don't know anything about it yet."

"Yes," Mary-Lou agreed, "but they'll also know that we've been found. I don't expect they'll have had very long to worry. Is there a spare roll? I've got a safe place for it if there is."

"It's getting dark," Rosemary said suddenly. "How will they see to work?"

"Oh, for that, they will have lights. They can take the batteries from cars and run the lights from them. I have heard of it being done in other rescues."

"Good!" Barbara said with emphasis. "I'm not grumbling, but I don't exactly want to spend another night here!" She paused to take a drink of the hot, sweet coffee before she continued, "Won't it be *paradisial* to go to bed between sheets? After a night on the floor, I can't imagine anything more heavenly."

95

At this point there came a splintering sound. A log in the roof shifted. There was a shout from the men working on it. Then a sudden gush of bitterly cold air poured into the hut as the log was slowly levered up and pushed aside. The girls cheered lustily, and Carol, who had a mouthful of roll at the time, choked and had to be patted on the back. But even she spluttered as soon as she could speak again, "Oh, thank goodness! They'll get us away tonight!"

They did; but it was dark and the skies were powdered with stars before Herr Tratschin was finally lowered into the hut. It was bitterly cold and everyone was shivering, but when they saw his broad, kindly face they all cheered loudly again. Their ordeal was ended, and soon they would be back at the farm.

"With hot baths, I hope," Mary-Lou said as she watched Herr Tratschin and another man who had joined him rope Naomi securely before they gave the signal, and she was drawn slowly up through the roof. "I'm filthier than I've ever been before, even in my wild youth! I'll be sorry for Frau Tratschin's sheets if we have to go to bed unbathed!"

One by one they went up on the ropes until they reached the broad ledge from which the men had been working. Great toboggans stood there, and they were packed in, and then a man bore each load away, pulling until he came to an opening between two great rocks, when he sat down, kicked off, and they went skimming over the snow which here was untouched by the avalanche, down—down—down, until they were flying across the plain to stop near a little encampment where each girl was seized on by a mistress from the school, hugged vehemently and then hurried away to where enormous sleighs, drawn by horses were waiting. By midnight, everyone was safe in bed. Matron ordained a full day's rest for everyone concerned, and further, kept Naomi, Verity, Barbara and Mary-Lou in bed until the end of the week, just to make sure. But after that, and when all parents had been heard from and knew that the girls were safe and sound, the school heaved a sigh of relief and returned to its normal activities.

"But I hope," Miss Annersley said when all the staff were at coffee on the Sunday night, "that that will prove the last of our trials for this term. If there is much more of this my hair will be white by Easter, and you had better book a place for me at the nearest mental hospital!"

Chapter 12

LOST PROPERTY

"WELL, it was all very exciting and might have been a lot worse, but I hope it's the last excitement we have to worry about until St. Mildred's panto," Mary-Lou remarked a week later when the two Sixths were enjoying life together in the common room.

"That won't be *our* excitement," Vi remarked as she handed round a box of fudge.

"No; that's so. Scarlet fever has done every last one of us out of taking part in it. This year we shall be merely audience for once."

"A welcome change," Prunella said with decision. "I've had all the thrills I want for one term, thank you!"

"I wonder what tale they've chosen?" Verity observed.

"Goodness knows! They never let us know until the last minute," Hilary reminded her.

However, they didn't have long to wait. On the Saturday morning a large notice appeared on the noticeboard in Hall.

"GRAND ANNUAL PANTOMIME!
PUSS IN BOOTS
To take place in St. Luke's Hall
on the afternoon of Tuesday, April 1st.
Volunteers to sell programmes and refreshments and
to act as usherettes will be welcome."

Beneath was a note in Miss Wilson's characteristic hand: "Members of VIa and b alone may apply."

"*Puss in Boots*! Well, that's a change, anyhow," Prunella commented when they had a spare moment together. "I wonder who will be 'Puss'?"

"It's a gorgeous part, if I remember the story right," Josette said.

"I bet your Sybil will be the 'Princess'," Barbara observed. "She's the St. Mildred Beauty Queen."

"I wish she could hear you!" Sybil's sister said feelingly. "She *would* tell you where you got off!"

"I should just think so!" Vi exclaimed. "You're right there, Josette! To hear her talk, sometimes, you'd think it was a positive crime to be pretty."

"Yes; I've noticed that," Hilary agreed. "I've always meant to ask what was at the bottom of it. Do you know, Jo?"

Josette shook her head. "Haven't the foggiest. I only know the quickest way to make her absolutely raging is to comment on her looks. She's always been like that, so far as I can remember."

"You're her sister; you ought to know," Hilary agreed. "A kink in her character, I expect. Oh, well, that's better than if she was all upstage about her beauty—for she *is* really lovely, you know. You and young Ailie aren't a patch on her, Josette, and you're neither of you exactly plain."

Before Josette could think of a sufficiently biting reply, the bell rang and they had to hurry off to classes again, so the subject was dropped.

During the evening preparation period, Mary-Lou, who had been having a special history coaching arrived in the prefects' room to demand with some indignation if anyone had seen her fountain pen or biro.

"I had to take notes in pencil and the point was blunt, and goodness knows if I can read half that I got down!" she complained bitterly.

No one knew anything about either. Doris Hill suggested

that she must have left them in either the library or the geography room.

"I didn't," Mary-Lou said. "I've been there to see, and they're nowhere about. Miss Moore was in geography, and she said they hadn't been brought to her and she'd seen nothing of them. I can't imagine myself being such a goop as to leave them lying around there, anyhow. I *don't* scatter my belongings broadcast!"

This was true, but, as Lesley Malcolm pointed out, the best of us may forget at times. "You'd better ask Josette," she added. "She's library pree. She's down in Lower IVb tonight, in case you don't know."

"I'll go; but I'm positive I left them both in my case after that lecture we had on Shelley from the Head," Mary-Lou replied, leaving the room to seek Josette and ask her if she knew anything about the missing articles.

"I haven't seen them myself," Josette said, thankfully giving up work on a very sticky piece of geometry. "No one has brought them to me, either. But it isn't like you to leave things around, Mary-Lou. What have you been doing? And that reminds me. Have you looked in Lost Propery?"

"I have not. In fact I'd forgotten about it, it's so long since I had anything there," Mary-Lou responded. "However, I can't find them anywhere else, and no one seems to have seen anything of them, so I'd better go and look, I suppose, though it's a last hope, I may tell you. Thanks a lot, Josette. Sorry to have interrupted you."

"Oh don't mind me. I was only too thankful for a break!" Josette retorted. "I've got the nastiest piece of geometry I've had all this term."

Mary-Lou laughed and went off to demand the key of Lost Property from Vi, who, as Second Prefect, always had charge of it.

"Lost Property? You *must* be desperate if you're reduced to hunting there!" Vi said, getting up from the table in the prefects' room. "OK. I'll go and fetch it. It's in my bureau—

for safety's sake. You trot along to the cupboard and wait for me. I shan't be more than a minute or two."

Mary-Lou went along to stand opposite the cupboard dedicated to Lost Property, while Vi ran off to her cubicle to get the key. She came down to find her friend awaiting her with a good deal of impatience.

"What an age you've been! Remember, I've had coaching since prep began, and so far I've scarcely done a thing!"

"Sorry, but I couldn't find it at first. It had shifted itself somehow to the very back of the drawer, and I had to fish under everything before I found it," Vi explained as she inserted the key and turned it.

The door did not wait to be pulled open. It simply *burst* open and at once an avalanche of mixed belongings cascaded from the shelves. Blazers, berets, gloves, books, pencil cases, pens, pencils and erasers tumbled out, not to mention a workbasket, the lid of which had fallen open so that it discharged its contents everywhere. Reels of cotton went rolling gaily down the corridor, followed by a thimble. Skeins of darning-wool and silk fell in every direction and packets of needles and pins, a pair of scissors and a bag of toffees showered over the rest. Mary-Lou had to chase one enterprising reel to the far end of the corridor before she caught up with it.

"What on earth . . ." she began as she came back. Then she interrupted herself. "Heavens! Here's that snap-album Lesley Bethune was bemoaning all yesterday! How on earth did it get here?"

"And here are Naomi's beloved Patience cards," Vi added, picking up the little case. The next moment, she dropped it to swoop down on a small brooch. "My tennis badge! How on earth did it get here? I haven't been wearing it lately."

"This," said Mary-Lou, the light of battle in her eyes, "is someone's idea of a joke. This blazer is Prunella's—here's the name tape. And this is Hilda's scarf. Oh, and my old purse that I keep stamps in!"

"But who under the sun would be such a complete idiot?" Vi demanded with some point as she stirred up the mess on the floor. "Gracious! Here's Lesley Malcolm's protractor and Hilary's gym shoes." She stood up and surveyed the pile with blazing eyes. Then she swung round on the Head Girl. "You're right, Mary-Lou! Someone has had the unbounded *sauce* to interfere with our things—for quite half the stuff here belongs to one or other of the Sixths. What are you going to do about it?"

Mary-Lou had listened to her in silence, and a grimmer expression spread over her face than most people had ever seen there before. "Do about it? When we've found out who is reponsible for this latest piece of idiocy, I propose to make whoever it is sorry that she—or they—was ever born! There's a limit to the practical jokes that can be played in this establishment, and they've gone well beyond it this time. I'll go and fetch one of the packing trays and we'd better clear all this lot up."

"Right! You scram and I'll do what I can—though, honestly," Vi added, "I just don't know where to begin, there's such a hotch-potch here!"

Mary-Lou giggled and fled, and Vi, squatting on the floor, began to sort things out. Certainly, as she reflected, whoever had been responsible seemed to have gone through all the rooms with vim. In fact, as she shrewdly suspected, this affair was the work of quite a number of people. One or even two girls could hardly have been responsible for such a collection!

Mary-Lou returned a few minutes later with one of the light wicker trays they used for unpacking, to find Vi surveying the heap of belongings thoughtfully. "I say, Mary-Lou! Has it ever struck you that whoever did this must have been at my drawers?"

"*What*? What on earth do you mean?"

"What I say. Think a sec. Where do I keep the key? In my hanky-box under the hankies. At least, it's always in that drawer. I won't vouch for it's always being in the box."

Mary-Lou's lips tightened into a straight line. "*That* sort of thing must stop pronto! They know, down to the newest Junior, that you don't go meddling with other folks' drawers. But that would account for the ages you took to find the thing. Probably whoever did it just shoved the key back anyhow when they'd finished with it. For you know, Vi, this isn't the work of *one* person. It's a lot too—too comprehensive for that!"

"I'd got as far as that myself," Vi assented, and turned back to her sorting. She brandished a bunch of pens, pencils and biros. "Better look through these and see if yours are here. Who do you think is responsible?"

"I don't know, but I'm jolly well going to make it my business to find out."

"*Poor* kids! I wouldn't be in their shoes for all the tea in China! That's fairly sorted out now, I think. Let's take this lot to our own room. Then we'd better get down to work."

The pair quickly filled the tray with the various heaps, and then bore it off to the prefects' room. They had expected to find one or two, at least, of their confrères there, but it was empty. They set the tray down, and then Mary-Lou glanced at her watch. The yelp she let out startled Vi, who asked anxiously what was wrong *now*?

"It's half-past eighteen and we ought to be down in the library for extra French! Come on! Look as apologetic as you can! We don't want to have to explain too much to Mdlle until we've gone into conference about this."

Mercifully for them Mdlle herself had been detained, and by the time she arrived in the library with apologies for her tardy arrival, the pair were in their places and looking, as Hilary said later, as if butter wouldn't melt in their mouths! After the lecture, the prefects gathered up their possessions and trooped off upstairs to their room to go on with their work, all unwitting of the fact that so far as lessons were concerned, little work would be done by them *that* evening.

Chapter 13

PREFECTS IN COUNCIL

"—AND all I've got to say is that, if I've got to remember all those writers of the Revolutionary period and their ... My sainted aunt Sempronia! *What's all this?*"

Hilary, talking as she went, flung open the door of the prefects' room, and stopped dead, staring with eyes that looked ready to drop out of her head at the piled-up tray Mary-Lou and Vi had planted on the table.

At her words, the pair responsible grinned at each other. The rest pressed forward to see what on earth had happened to cause such amazement.

"What—on—earth——" Lesley Bethune began, but was interrupted by Prunella, who leapt forward with a cry of, "My blazer! How on earth did it get here? I left it on my peg. Who's been doing what to make it look as if I'd gone to bed for a week in it?"

Hilda Jukes followed her. "And my scarf!"

Hilary swung round on Mary-Lou and Vi. "You two! This is your doing. Oh, not the collection, idiots! But you two brought it here! What's the meaning of it?"

Mary-Lou slid round the excited throng and took her place at the head of the table. "Keep calm—keep calm—all of you! As for what's been going on and who's been doing what, will all of you please take a dekko at this lot and bag anything of yours among them. Here's your snap-album for one, Lesley. And your gym shoes are there, Hilary."

The prefects goggled at the miscellaneous heaps in silence. Then Hilary picked up her gym shoes and that broke the spell. They surged forward and for a moment or two cries and exclamations sounded as they found belongings that some of them had never even missed. Finally, Hilary, still staring as if she could not believe her senses, demanded, "What does it mean, anyhow? Where did you get this lot?"

"From Lost Property," Mary-Lou said blandly.

"But," Lesley Bethune cried loudly, "how on earth did it all get there? The only thing *I've* put there this week was Richenda Fry's umbrella, which I found sculling about loose in their Splashery instead of being hung on her peg."

"And I haven't had a thing," Doris Hill added. "Besides, if you come to that, will you explain how my geom. instruments came there? To my certain knowledge I put them away properly yesterday and I haven't had them out since."

Prunella, having pulled on her blazer, turned to the Head Girl. "What's the meaning of it, Mary-Lou?"

"Best sit down," Mary-Lou said, pulling out a chair and setting the example. "Now then, all of you, lend me your ears. And keep any comments until I've finished. Someone— or several someones, for I don't for a moment think that *one* girl is responsible for the size of this lot—has thought it funny to go round gathering up things regardless. Then, if you please, someone must have gone to Vi's cubey and helped herself to Lost Property key and shoved the whole lot in."

Mary-Lou's voice was very quiet, but her eyes glinted like pieces of steel, and the listening prefects realised that she was furiously angry. If it came to that, they were angry themselves. Many of the things they had rescued could only have been taken from their desks or pegs or Splashery lockers, and that was a piece of impudence that had not happened before.

Hilary spoke first. "Do you really mean that they had the *cheek* to go to Vi's drawers and help themselves! Who would do such a thing? I can quite well see that some mindless wenches might think it funny to shove the things into Lost

Property if the door were open already—and," she added in parenthesis, "I'd like to know how they ever managed to get it shut again on that lot!—but surely no one would do a thing like that?"

"Obviously they did it, since the thing was done," Vi said. She, too, was plainly very angry. Her deep, violet-blue eyes were flashing in a way few people had ever seen them flash, and her pretty mouth was a straight line. She had had time to realise the cool impudence of the business, and though, like Mary-Lou, she was quiet outwardly, inwardly she was raging.

There was a silence. Then Hilda Jukes, a big, good-natured girl whom no one had ever seen out of temper before throughout her whole school career, spoke with an edge to her voice that gave them all a fresh shock.

"This is beyond a joke! I hope when you find out who did it, you'll make them smart for it, Mary-Lou. We'll all back you up, whatever you suggest! We can't have that sort of thing going on. It's downright cheek and none too honest, either."

"Don't you worry! When we've discovered who it is we'll give them a lesson they'll remember to their last day!" Mary-Lou retorted. "Look here! It's getting on for Abendessen. Make sure you've got all your own things, and then we'll dispose of this lot. Prefects' meeting after Abendessen, all of you!"

Once more the prefects turned their attention to the heaps of oddments. Two or three things such as fountain pens and biros had been overlooked and were now claimed.

Mary-Lou, rather calmer now, took charge. "Well, if you're all sure you've got everything that's yours, I vote we shove the rest into the bottom of the cupboard. Give me a hand, someone. Open the doors, will you, Vi?"

Vi opened the double doors at the bottom of the huge cupboard in which the prefects kept their private belongings, and Mary-Lou and Hilary lifted the tray and pushed it gently in on the floor, where it just fitted in.

During Abendessen, the prefects, though they talked lightly among themselves, were mainly occupied in regarding the younger girls carefully. Remembering her own impish day, Mary-Lou had an idea that the perpetrators would probably be keeping an eye on on the prefects to see if they could find out whether or not the grandees of the school knew about it yet.

"Thank goodness for that, anyhow!" Hilary, who sat next to her, muttered.

Mary-Lou started. "Thank goodness for what?"

"I was watching the IVa folk to see if any of them looked self-conscious or were extra giggly, and I can't see that they're any worse than usual. Heather Warner and Connie Winter have been tittering, but that's nothing fresh for them. No; IVa are out of it all right."

"I was at the same game myself," Mary-Lou said when she had finished her soup. "I've absolved both Upper Fourths. But I'm by no means so sure of Lower. Ailie Russell has been squinting across at us whenever she thought we weren't looking, and so has Janice Chester. Those two are demons, and they never bother to think, but do whatever mad idea enters their silly heads on the instant."

"Gosh! If young Ailie is in it won't Madame be mad if she ever hears of it!" murmured Hilary, referring to Lady Russell who had established the school when it was in Tirol. She was far too busy these days. Her three girls, Sybil, now at St. Mildred's, and Josette and Ailie had naturally become pupils at the first possible moment. If Ailie really had any hand in the stealing of Vi's key, and her mother ever heard of it, she certainly would be furious.

Doris Hill, sitting at Mary-Lou's other hand, had overheard their talk. She leaned across the table to Hilary. "If it's that crowd, it's simply an extra bad attack of insanity," she said in low tones. "We can deal with that all right!"

107

Mary-Lou was looking relieved. "So long as it isn't any of the Senior Middles! But you're right, of course, Doris. With that crew, it's merely spring madness. Bless their little hearts! They're for it, all right! We'll see to it that whatever else they may do they'll never play that joke again—or not in this place!" Her eyes went across to the table where the members of Lower IVa were sitting, and Ailie Russell, stealing a furtive look across at *her* at the same moment, caught the look and turned scarlet.

"What's wrong with you?" demanded one of her two boon companions, Janice Chester.

"That Mary-Lou, drat her!" Ailie muttered under her breath. "I say, Jan, I rather think they know. She was staring over here looking like—like the Judgment Day!"

After that the pair kept their eyes on their own table, but Mary-Lou had seen Ailie's look though she had not seen the colour sweep over the small face under its fair curls, and she was almost sure in her own mind now that Lower IV knew all about the affair. She promptly dismissed the whole thing from her mind and began to chat in her ordinary manner. Those members of VIb who were not prefects, but sat at the same table had been feeling the constraint and wondered what was at the bottom of it. Now, thanks to Mary-Lou's sudden return to insouciance, it vanished, and everyone breathed more freely.

Prayers came immediately after Abendessen, and after Prayers, though the Juniors went off to bed, the rest had a free period when they might amuse themselves as they chose so long as they were quiet. On this evening the three Fifths and two Upper Fourths remained in Hall for dancing, Mddle Lenoir, the junior music mistress having consented to play for them. The two Lower Fourths retired to their common room, and Mary-Lou, looking rather like a cat who has stolen the cream, so bland was her expression, invited what was left of VIb to the prefects' room, where the story was

108

unfolded to them and they were invited to hunt for their own possessions on the wicker tray.

"Who's responsible for all this 'ere?" Virginia Adams asked flippantly.

"We can't be sure, but we rather suspect the Lower Fourths," the Head Girl said. "Naomi, your Patience cards are there, for I saw them. Have you found them?"

Naomi nodded. "They were right on top. What are you going to do about it?"

"Hold a meeting and discuss it first. One thing I can promise you people. When we've done with whoever it is we won't hear a peep out of them for a long time to come. It was cheek of the worst to touch any of our things, especially as they must have taken things that were in their proper places all right. Don't you worry. They'll be told exactly where they get off, I promise you!"

Clare Kennedy looked up suddenly. "You know, Mary-Lou, I rather think this is an effort to get back on us because we have been so strict about untidiness."

"Do you really think so?" Mary-Lou asked.

Jessica Wayne assented to this. "If you ask me, they're lumping the whole of us Sixths together. I know I ticked Janice Chester off good and hard for leaving her shoes lying in the middle of the Splashery floor, and she had the cheek to say, 'You're not a pree, so it's none of your business!' I nearly ate her without salt," she added reflectively.

Hilary rose from her seat. "I know we aren't having a regular prees' meeting at this moment, but I should like to put a suggestion to all prees, just the same."

"What is it?" The question came from seven people at once.

"That we co-opt the rest of Lower Sixth for this affair. Look!" she went on eagerly. "It's nearly the end of this term. There's one more to go, and then where shall *we* all be? Most of us at St. Mildred's, I know; but the others are leaving school altogether. So how about starting the non-prefects in

VIb by bringing them in on this? It ought to be a help to them when they have to step into our shoes, you know. And they can probably help us by making suggestions about how to deal with those young demons."

Mary-Lou pursed up her mouth. "Can we do it without going to the Abbess first, do you think?"

"I think we can," Vi put in. "Oh, I expect we'll have to let her know all about it later—off the record, of course."

"OK then. Seeing you're all here, find chairs and sit round the table and let's get to business. You folk will have to get seats from other rooms. I don't think we've anything like enough to seat all of you."

There was a bustle, and, ten minutes later, they were all crowded round the table with the non-prefects from VIb looking extra portentous at this unexpected responsibility that had been thrust on them.

"Well," Mary-Lou said, rising when they were all ready, "there's no need to explain why we're having this meeting. You all know the reason, so I think we'd better set to work at once and discover how we can best deal with it. The meeting is open for discussion." Then she sat down and looked round them expectantly.

Prunella got up at once—with some difficulty, they were sitting so close together. "I don't think we need bother about either of the Upper IV forms," she said. "I've had an eye on them, and I honestly don't think they know a thing about it."

"I think you're right there," Mary-Lou agreed. "It's the Lowers we have to consider—especially that gang that Ailie Russell leads."

"If Ailie and Judy are in it, Janice certainly will be," Barbara said gloomily. "Those three always hunt together."

"What a little ass she is!" her cousin Vi remarked frankly. "Didn't Uncle Peter say that if she got into any more major rows here he'd take her away and send her back to Carnbach for another year?"

"He did—and I shouldn't be sorry, either!" Barbara said fervently. "Mummy would be furious with her if that happened, and so would Beth. Bethy always says she had a fairly blameless record at school, and I haven't done anything very bad. If young Jan spoils our record, she'll get it in the neck on all sides. And the worst of it is Daddy seems to think I ought to keep more of an eye on her! As if *I* could stop her behaving like an imp of darkness!"

"Order—order!" Mary-Lou cried. "Just confine yourselves to the business in hand, please."

Hilary stood up. "I should like to propose, Madam Chairman, that we call a meeting of those two forms and ask them who was responsible for the latest."

"I'll second that!" Lesley Malcolm cried.

"There's one blessing!" Hilda Jukes said. "They won't try to lie about it. They're imps of the first water, but they *are* honest."

"How are you going to deal with them when you've found out who it is?" Naomi asked suddenly.

Mary-Lou turned to her quickly. "I don't think any of us have got that far. Have you any ideas, Naomi? If so, for goodness sake trot them out! Lines won't meet the case, nor black marks, either. And I don't want to fine them if it can be helped. Besides," she added frankly, "I'd rather like to make the punishment fit the crime if we possibly can."

Naomi flushed. "I've got an idea, but it mightn't work."

"Tell us what it is," Vi urged. "Quite likely it's just the thing. Go ahead, Naomi! We're all waiting."

Naomi went pinker than ever. "I'll tell you; but if you think it's mad, mind you say so. I shan't mind. Only what Mary-Lou said about making the punishment fit the crime—well, I rather think it *might*."

"Oh, go on!" Clare implored. "You're working us all up by this mystery. What *is* your idea?"

Naomi spoke then for a space of five minutes. When she stopped, everyone else clapped loud and long.

"It's a honey!" Hilary exclaimed. "As you say, it does, exactly, fit the crime, and they'll simply loathe doing it. Besides, everyone concerned will tell them their exact opinion of them—including our noble selves. And that reminds me. We all claimed our own things, didn't we? We'll have to put them back again."

"What? But I can't do without my pen or my biro!" Mary-Lou cried.

"Well put one back, then. But they've got to have something for each of us or we shan't get *our* chance. Believe me, I'm looking forward to it. Just let me once get my claws into those little whatnots and they'll be sorry they ever were born!"

In the end it was decided that every single member of the two Sixths must put something on the tray. When that was done, the bell rang for bed, and they hurriedly set the room to rights before they all trooped off to the dormitories.

Naomi, limping along, was overtaken by Clare and Jessica Wayne.

"You really are a genius, Naomi!" Jessica declared. "I'll bet anything you like that once this business is over that gang will be as meek as Moses for the rest of the term!"

Naomi blushed and then laughed. "I hope so, I'm sure. But there's no genius about it, Jessica. I only thought what I should most hate myself if I were in their shoes and that came like a flash."

They had reached the dormitory then, so she said goodnight as Clare and Jessica were in another. But as she slowly undressed and got ready for bed, she realised that she was beginning to feel one with the others—something she had not done for a good many years now. Mary-Lou's straight talk had started her off on a new path. This business of the Juniors looked like being a long step forward.

"I was mad about my cards," she thought when she was finally in bed, "but now I'm not so sure I don't feel like blessing those imps. And—and I'll do as Mary-Lou wants.

I'll ask Dr. Maynard if he thinks anything can be done about me. And—and . . . ."

But here she suddenly stopped thinking, and acted. Very solemnly she prayed with all her heart that this new happiness which seemed to be coming to her might help her for the future to be like other girls in some things if not all.

Chapter 14

NEMESIS ARRIVES

"MAY you have the two Lower Fourths for inquisition immediately after Kaffee und Kuchen this afternoon?" Miss Annersley sat up in her big armchair and eyed her Head Girl with interest. "What have those young monkeys been doing now?"

"I'd rather not say, if you don't mind, please," Mary-Lou replied, standing very tall and upright in her winter evening frock of deep blue velveteen.

"And why not, pray?" But there was an amused look in the keen blue-grey eyes surveying the girl.

"Because it's something we feel it might be better to handle ourselves. You see," Mary-Lou continued with the stunning frankness they had all come to expect from her, but which still could take away the breath of the person treated to it, "if we hand it over to you, you'll feel bound to take notice of it, and—well—well—the St. Mildred pantomime is awfully close at hand."

"I see." Miss Annersley smiled. "Are you sure it's something you can deal with yourselves quite adequately?"

"Oh, *yes*!" Mary-Lou replied with such fervour that the Head broke into a peal of laughter. "I promise you they'll think a hundred times before they embark on such doings again."

Miss Annersley recovered herself. "That sounds portentous! Very well, Mary-Lou. I'll be quite pleased to be saved from pronouncing any very heavy judgments at this late

114

date. You may have them. By the way, it's nothing really *bad*?"

Mary-Lou grinned. "Not bad—merely mischief and un-heard-of cheek!"

"Then in that case, by all means settle it yourselves. But don't forget I shall expect to hear the whole story when it's all over—off the record, of course."

Mary-Lou chuckled. "Oh, you shall—you certainly shall! It would be much too good to keep from you in those condi-tions. Anyhow, Auntie Joey is to hear of it. She hasn't been feeling awfully well this last week or two, Len tells me, and she loves to hear any *startling* school news. I'm going to tea with her on Sunday, you remember, and I hope to give her the whole yarn then. I know perfectly well that she'll spill the beans to you sooner or later—er—I mean tell you." She amended her sentence in some confusion. "But it *will* be off the record, won't it? I mean, we don't want to mess up their reports."

"Off the record," the Head promised solemnly, her eyes dancing. "And while I think of it, be a little more careful of your language, please. You can't very well pull up the younger girls for slang if you are perpetually using it your-self."

"No; it would be a case of Satan rebuking Satan, I supose," Mary-Lou said cheerfully. "I'll be careful—we all are in public. Thank you, Miss Annersley. I'd better go now. The gong will sound for Kaffee und Kuchen in three minutes, and I'm on urn duty this afternoon."

"Off you go, then. Come along here after the Middles have gone to bed—all of you, I mean—and let me know the latest. I'll have coffee and biscuits."

"Oh, thank you; that will be gorgeous. I'll tell the rest." Mary-Lou turned to leave the room, but before she had reached the door she was called back.

"Oh—one moment, Mary-Lou! While you're about it, you might improve the occasion with a few remarks on general tidiness. Quite half Vb turned up at my lesson this morning minus either writing materials or textbooks. If it wasn't one thing, it was another. I'm not going to pass that sort of thing, and it might come better from you prefects than me. See to it, please."

Mary-Lou reddened, rather to the Head's surprise. "I'll see to it," she promised hurriedly before she bobbed her curtsey and made good her escape.

"Whew! That was a near touch!" she thought as she hurried along to the main building where the Speisesaal was. "Hope I didn't give anything away by going red in that idiotic way. The Abbess is always so appallingly on the spot!"

She entered the Speisesaal where Clare, Verity and Hilary were already busy at the big urns, filling the long rows of cups with steaming coffee. She nodded to them as she entered, and went to take her place at the remaining one.

"The Head has agreed?" Verity asked eagerly.

"Oh, yes; but we knew she would. She's always reasonable. The only thing is, she insists on hearing all about it off the record. We're all to go and have coffee and biscuits with her after the Middles' bedtime. But she did give me rather a jolt as I was coming out. She asked me to say something about tidiness. Half Vb had to turn up at her lesson minus their belongings. I couldn't explain then, of course, so it looked like being rather awkward."

"What did you do?" Hilary demanded.

"Told her I'd see to it, and *ran*. There goes the gong! This subject must now drop!" And she turned her back on the others, and applied herself to filling the empty cups at top speed.

Unaware of the excitement that awaited them, the school filed in, marched up to their appointed urns to take their cups, and went to their places at table. The prefects finished their job, carried off their own cups, and sat down to enjoy rolls and butter, fancy bread-twists and buns.

"What exactly did the Head say?" Vi asked when the meal was well begun and everyone else was far too busy to pay much heed to the prefects.

"Oh, asked if I was sure we could deal adequately with the situation. I said we could, and she said she wasn't sorry as she didn't want to have to administer any heavy justice at this late date."

"Trust her!" Vi said in a tone full of affection. "There isn't much that she misses, is there? Well, you did say we must tell Auntie Joey the whole yarn when we went to tea with her on Sunday, and if she knows, it won't be long before the Abbess and Bill know, so I suppose they may as well hear it firsthand from us."

"When are you going to warn the little wretches?" Doris asked.

"As soon as this is over. I don't want to spoil their meal. They'll need all the support they can get from it!" Mary-Lou chuckled.

"I'm sorry for them from the bottom of my heart," Clare observed, looking her saintliest. "Mind you rub it well in! We don't want any more bothers of this kind next term. I don't suppose they'll feel like anything but behaving themselves for the rest of *this*, once they've finished."

"Don't worry! I'll see to that, all right!" Mary-Lou said grimly.

The meal was not quite ended when she sipped the last of her coffee, put down her cup, and rose to clap her hands for attention. The buzz of chatter and laughter died down at once, and everyone turned to look at the prefects' table, most of them with surprise.

"All girls from Lower IVa and b will remain behind after the tables are cleared," the Head Girl said, her clear, bell-like voice carrying to every corner of the room. "The rest of you, when you are finished, please hurry with the clearing and leave the room at once. That is all." She sat down again and shot a smile round the table, receiving answering smiles from everyone.

The greater part of the school remained silent for a moment or two from sheer surprise. Then the clatter began again. Only at the tables where the two Lower Fourths were congregated was there a marked lack of noise. One or two of the girls wondered aloud what Mary-Lou wanted with them; but several people looked suddenly blue and there were appetites to seek amongst them. In fact, it was noted then, and remarked on later, that Ailie Russell and her two satellites stopped eating, and Ailie would even have left half her bun on her plate if the Senior in charge had not reminded her of it.

"Eat your bun, Ailie," Rosamund Lilley said firmly. "And what have you people been doing now, I should like to know?"

She got no reply; she had hardly expected one, and had turned at once to continue with the light gossip she had been exchanging with her friend, Jo Scott. But Ailie looked like a thundercloud as she choked down her remnant of unwanted bun.

Judy Willoughby, seated next to her, nudged her. "Ailie! Do you think—"

"Oh, shut *up*! But I'd like to know how they got on to us. Who's squeaked?"

"No one has," said Janice Chester, a leggy eleven-year-old with straight black hair dropping in pigtails over either shoulder. "I *warned* you Mary-Lou would be on to us at once, and you said she wouldn't. Well, I was right!"

Ailie flushed angrily. "You always are, aren't you, Miss Knowall? I notice your ideas didn't keep you out of the fun, all the same."

Janice looked both hurt and surprised. "What did you expect? You two were in it, and when you *would* go on, I couldn't very well stand out against you all by myself, could I? We're *pals*!"

118

"Oh, well," Judy put in with some idea of smoothing things over, "it was a good joke on them, anyhow! I'll bet Vi got a shock when she opened Lost Property door!" She suddenly giggled. "The whole lot must have collapsed on her at once. It was all we could do to keep it in while we locked the door. I only wish I had been there to see it!"

Ailie's face lightened as she thought of that picture. "It must have been awfully funny," she admitted; and swallowed the last bite of bun.

All the same, they were not really sorry when Kaffee und Kuchen came to an end, and the rest, scurrying under the stern eyes of both Sixths, cleared the tables and then fled to make the most of the interval between the meal and preparation.

The two Lower Fourths had obediently gone back to their tables and sat down again. When the last of the other girls had left the Speisesaal, carefully closing the door behind her, Mary-Lou moved to the high table where the staff usually sat. They all eyed her apprehensively, even those whose consciences were fairly clear at the moment. *What* was going to happen?

She stood looking at them in silence with a pitying smile on her lips. The horrid pause lasted fully two minutes, by which time Ailie, at least, was on the verge of bursting into a wild yell. Then the Head Girl spoke.

"Which of you," she asked sweetly, "was responsible for cramming everything into Lost Property?"

Silence! Then Ailie gave a gulp that was little short of a whoop, and scrambled to her feet. At once her two main supporters got to theirs. From round the two tables sundry other people rose here and there until seven Junior Middles were finally standing, all with a hangdog expression which made Mary-Lou and some of the others bite their lips.

The Head Girl waited until it was clear that no one else was going to join the throng. Then she turned a piercing look on Ailie, whom she shrewdly guessed to have been the ring leader. "Is this all, Aline?" she asked.

The use of her full Christian name floored Ailie completely. "I—I think so!" she gasped.

"Don't you *know*?" Mary-Lou demanded.

"I—yes; it is," Ailie muttered.

Judy, not quite so upset, lifted up her voice. "I'm not *quite* sure that Janice ought to stand up, Mary-Lou," she said. "She didn't want us to do it one bit, and did all she knew to stop us. She said . . . ."

At this point the Head Girl looked straight at her with steely eyes, and she found herself finishing with an incoherent mutter, so none of the Sixth ever knew what it was that Janice had said. Mary-Lou continued to look until the young lady's head drooped and her long lashes swept her crimson cheeks. As for Janice, she opened her mouth to speak, and then thought better of it and closed it again.

Mary-Lou continued with her gaze for a full thirty seconds. Then she transferred it to the sitting girls. "In that case, as you folk have nothing to do with all this, you may go. Go quietly, please. Josette, you might see them through the corridors, if you will. You, too, Barbara. They are to go to their common room and stay there until the bell rings for prep. You two had better remain with them, I think, until whoever is in charge comes along. Do you mind?"

Thankful to be out of it, the two elder sisters got up and went to usher the major part of the two forms to their common room. As she went past the Lower IVa table, Josette deliberately turned on her small sister a look that almost literally froze that young woman. Barbara simply stalked past Janice without looking at her, and Janice was nearly reduced to tears. Mary-Lou waited until the party had gone. Then she turned her attention to the seven culprits.

"Come and stand up here—before the table," she said. "At once, please!"

120

There was the crack of a whip in her last words which made the seven hurriedly shuffle out of their places and come to stand in a straight line before the high table. Not one lifted her eyes, and when they got there they twisted their fingers madly together, shuffled their feet, and Janice, who was addicted in moments of stress to standing on one leg and rubbing the instep of the other foot up and down it, nearly overbalanced in her agitation. A more guilty-looking set of girls it would have been hard to find.

Mary-Lou did not spare them. "Well?" she said sharply. "What have you to say for yourselves?"

No one spoke, not even Judy the audacious. As that young person said later, it mightn't have been so bad if it had been only Mary-Lou or even just the prefects. But to have the whole of both Sixths sitting there, staring at them as if they were toads or slugs or adders simply didn't give you a chance to think of a thing you could say!

Hilary took a hand now. "You set of *crawling* insects!" she said—and the sinners cringed before her wrath—"how dared you do such a thing?"

"Yes," Vi cried. "And how dared you go to my drawers and rifle them for the key? Of all the disgusting, dishonour-able, dishonest things to do! Janice, I'm ashamed to think you are my cousin!"

At this diatribe, Janice found her voice—the only one to do it just then, for the rest merely tried to make themselves as small as possible and wished the floor would open and swallow them up.

"We didn't, Vi! We *never* did!" she cried indignantly. "We wouldn't do such a horrid thing!"

"Indeed? I am glad to know that even *you* seem to have your limits," Vi told her with such an edge to her voice, that her small cousin only just escaped bursting into tears on the spot.

Mary-Lou had been looking at them with an expression of mild curiosity that hurt when any of them ventured to glance up and see it. "Then how *did* you get the cupboard open?" she inquired. "I'm sorry to seem so unbelieving, but if you didn't go to Vi's drawers and help yourselves to her key, how did you manage? I'm only asking for information," she added kindly.

They could have done without her kindness. Every word she said brought home to them the enormity of their conduct and they didn't dare to think what might follow when sentence was pronounced. Janice gulped loudly, and Ailie only kept the tears back by blinking hard, gripping her fingers together until they hurt, and swallowing.

The information came from another member of the party, Tessa de Bersac, a French girl, and daughter of one of Joey Maynard's closest friends, once Simone Lecoutier of earlier annals of the school. In her agitation she forgot that it was an "English" day, and spoke in French. Mary-Lou cut her short.

"Repeat what you said in English, Tessa," Mary-Lou said severely.

Thus urged, Tessa stammered, "Mais—I only said—I said—th-that we were *not* dishonourable and—and we d-did not t-touch Vi's d-d-drawers." After which she burst into tears and wept loudly.

"Stop that!" Mary-Lou said very quietly, but with something in her tone that made the emotional Tessa gulp loudly and, producing a handkerchief that had seen distinctly better days, mop her eyes fiercely.

The bell rang for preparation, but no one took any notice of it. The Middles were far too overcome to heed anything but their own particular trouble, and the prefects were determined to finish up this business before they dismissed the seven.

Mary-Lou was silent while it was ringing. When it was dumb and the sounds of hurrying footsteps had died away, she returned to the charge once more.

"If you did *not* steal Vi's key," she said—and oh, how the

122

polite scepticism in her voice hurt!—"may I ask how you managed to get the door open?"

Ailie pulled herself together. "The—the key of the cupboard in our form room fits," she muttered, not daring to meet the Head Girl's eyes.

Mary-Lou gasped. This was something of which she had *not* thought. However, she recovered herself instantly. "I see. In that case, I must ask Matron to have the lock of your cupboard changed at once. We can scarcely trust you again."

The seven were all darkly crimson, but none of them ventured to say anything. She allowed her final remark to sink in. Then, after a quick look round her colleagues, she pronounced sentence.

"You are silly, empty-headed little girls. When you planned your great joke, you didn't even stop to think that if you got a Head's Report for this affair, it would mean that you would miss the pantomime."

She stopped there as seven separate gasps of horror answered this. They had *not* thought of it. In fact, they had forgotten all about the pantomime. Surely, this was not to be their fate?

"It would serve you all right if we *did* give you Reports, especially as you had the impudence to go to other people's desks and lockers and pegs and help yourselves from them!" Hilary interjected. "How Tessa can say that you are not dishonourable is more than I can say!"

They flinched before her righteous anger. One or two were clearly on the verge of tears and Mary-Lou decided that she might as well finish it up.

"We are not giving you Head's Reports," she said curtly. "Instead, we have decided that the best thing to do will be to see that you undo, as far as possible, the annoyance and inconvenience you have caused other people. First, your pocket money for the rest of the term will be confiscated to pay for the fines other people would have had to pay if all this had not been found out so soon."

"B-but . . . b-but . . ." stammered Judy, the only one of the seven with enough self-possession left to make any sort of reply to this horrid judgment.

'Be quiet, please. You have nothing to do but listen to what we have decided," Mary-Lou said severely. "I have not finished yet. Besides losing your pocket money, you will take all the things to which you helped yourselves and you will return them to their owners, apologising to each girl at the same time. I don't know just how you will explain yourselves," she added sweetly. "That is for you to consider. But that is what you will do. Furthermore, as soon as your prep is over, you will begin at once. Every single article has to be returned to its rightful owner before you go to bed tonight. If it makes you late, you can explain to Matron just *why* you are late. That is all."

She sat down and the appalled septette began slowly to realise the full awfulness of their punishment. Meanwhile, Vi and Doris had left the room quitely. They returned at this moment with the wicker tray piled high with all the oddments the giddy crew had thought it such fun to put into Lost Property. They could see no fun in it now.

Something snapped in Ailie at the sight. "We won't do it!" she exclaimed. "You've no right to try and make us—"

"We have *every* right," Lesley Bethune interrupted her. "Anyhow, it's that or a Head's Report."

"And be quick and make up your minds which it's to be," Prunella added. "*We* have work to do if *you* haven't. You've wasted quite enough of our time as it is with your silly ongoings!"

There would be no choice, of course, in spite of Ailie's outburst. Not one of them would willingly have missed the pantomime, not to mention all the other dreadful penalties attached to a Report. The seven began to weep like waterspouts. Not that it got them anything but an admonition to stop at once and go and make the best use they could of what was left of their prep time.

"We'll carry this thing to Lower IVa for you," Mary-Lou said. "As soon as the bell goes for the end of prep, you may begin at once to sort it out and return the things. One of us will come and oversee the sorting for you. And remember! you are to apologise fully and properly to every one you have victimised."

Judy mopped her eyes and raised a timid hand. "Please, Mary-Lou, what does 'victimise' mean?" she asked.

Mary-Lou nearly choked with sudden laughter. She had forgotten Judy's passion for new words. However, she made a wild clutch at her vanishing gravity and replied stonily, "'made a victim of'. Now go and wash your faces and then straight to prep. You've less than half-an-hour left," she added.

They fled in short order. But the less said about their work that evening the better. Every single one of them found herself with at least one returned lesson next day and most of them with the lot. Apart from that, Janice and Ailie had to face the wrath of elder sisters who did not spare their tongues when they got them alone. All the same, every single article had been returned to its owner by bedtime, though the work kept them going until the bell rang and, in fact, three of them would have been in trouble with Matron for coming upstairs late if that lady had not been on the telephone for ten minutes after they were due in their cubicles. They had to make the apologies and quite a number of people told them exactly what they thought of them before they let them go. However, the nastiest part of their punishment was over when the last handkerchief had been claimed. After that, it seemed to matter very little that they must be penniless for the last fortnight or more of term. But it is on record that never again did the seven play such a joke. The results of the first had been too awful!

Chapter 15

THE UNEXPECTED

"WELL," Joey Maynard said as she sat down in the most comfortable chair in Miss Annersley's pretty drawing-room, "I only hope that's going to be the last."

"The last of what?" Miss Wilson queried, bringing her a cup of coffee.

"The last of our trials, of course. Goodness knows, this term has been chock-a-block with them. I don't know about you folk, but I'm at the stage where I'd like to lie back and take life easily for the next few weeks. What with scarlet fever and avalanches—"

"There was only *one* of that!" Nancy Wilmot pointed out.

"One too many, if you ask me. And don't interrupt. It's most horribly rude!"

"Poor old Joey!" Nancy said, laughing. "It *has* taken you badly! Never mind, though. I don't see what can go wrong in the last week or two of this term which, I don't mind owning, has been more than the outside of enough! About everything that could go wrong has done it. But there's only the St. Mildred's pantomime left, and that, thank goodness, is not our affair."

"No; but it's ours," Miss Wilson reminded her.

"True for you. By the way, are you going to let us into the secret of how you are going to manage when you have to provide the entire cast?"

"Not I! You may wait for the night. It will," Miss Wilson said very primly, "be a good exercise in patience for all of you."

"Isn't she maddening?" Joey murmured. "I vote we change the subject. What's the news of Rosalie? She hasn't done much about letter-writing since she went."

"Oh, she's completely cured now. I had a letter from Evvy yesterday," Peggy Burnett said. "Rosalie has regained all her old colour and weight and is eating well and sleeping well, and looks a different creature from the washed-out object she took away with her. They're coming back for the panto, they hope."

Nancy Wilmot looked up from her knitting. "I had a letter, too, and if you ask me, I should say something's been happening. Evvy was—well—*mysterious*."

"In what way?" Joey sat up and looked interested.

"I couldn't tell you. It was more what she said than what she didn't."

Joey chuckled. "If Evvy's taken to being mysterious, wild horses won't drag any sense out of her. I know that much."

The pantomime was always a matinee for the sake of those folk who might not be out-of-doors, once night had fallen. St. Luke's Hall stood at the gates of the great Sanatorium of which Jack Maynard was head, and quite a number of people from the villages round made the trip to enjoy the girls' production. All the Seniors had volunteered to act as usherettes, sell programmes and see to the refreshments they always had during the intervals. Apart from them, of the school proper, only members of the orchestra were taking part this year, thanks to the scarlet fever outbreak. St. Mildred's had had to revise all their plans in a hurry and handle everything else for themselves. They had gone about with pleased smirks for the past three weeks, and, which maddened the rest more than anything else, there was no getting any information out of the orchestra. As a result, the school at large was on tiptoe with expectation, and when, at last, they set off they were all wild with excitement.

Arrived at the hall, those helping in the front of the house departed to get their orders and the rest filed into their places, pulled off berets and coats and waited impatiently for their programmes. They were wildly curious by this time to know how St. Mildred's had contrived to manage without their help. A concerted groan arose when they found that the cunning "Millies" had merely listed the names of the characters without saying who was playing what.

"Cheatery!" cried Hilary, surveying the list with disgust.

"I wonder just who they've roped in to help?" Mary-Lou said thoughtfully.

"I don't see who they *could* get," Vi chimed in. "Well, we'll just have to hold our horses till the curtain goes up, I suppose." Then Joey came sailing down the aisle with her small Cecil in her arms and the twins trotting gaily in front of her. The girls gave it up, and turned to welcome her joyfully.

"Where are you sitting, Auntie Jo?" Josette demanded.

"Cecil and I are going to sit at the back with the staff just in case she demands to be taken out," Joey explained. "I'm leaving the twins in front of you folk, and you can keep an eye on them among you." She turned to the pair. "In you go, in front of Josette and—Naomi, isn't it? It's not like me not to know the new girls, Naomi, but this has been such a term, there hasn't been a single chance for you to come over to Freudesheim. However, we can alter that next term. Now, twins, listen to me a moment. Felix, you are *not* to talk while the play is going on. Save up your remarks for the intervals, please. Felicity, if you want to go out, wait till then, also, and then ask Josette to take you."

The milk-fair twins nodded solemnly, and promised that they would be good.

"Can I have my sweeties, please?" Felix demanded.

"Here you are." Joey put a bag into his fat hands, and gave one to Felicity. "Marshmallows for my girl and toffees for you, Felix." She turned to the girls. "Please, all of you, don't offer them any of yours. They have enough, and I don't want to spend the night attending to bilious babes! They may each have an ice in the first interval, but that's all. See to it,

128

Josette, will you?" She cast a somewhat harassed look at her twins, and then retired with Cecil to seek her own seat beside the Head.

"Give me Cecil," that lady said. "How she is growing! Quite a big girl for two! And Con's miniature!"

"Yes, isn't she?" Joey agreed, handing her over and sitting down. "Con's fearfully proud of that. She and Cecil are the only really dark members of my family so far. Now let me see this programme we've heard so much about." She laughed as she opened it, and looked mischievous. "The girls haven't a clue, you know! I heard them when I parked the twins just now."

Miss Annersley laughed, too. "Don't I know it! They're all bursting to know what it means and no one would give them a hint."

She got no further, for at that moment, a slim, very elegant young woman came down the side aisle to stop and gaze round, and then pause beside Joey with the remark, "Hi, Joey! I guess you didn't think we'd make it, but here we are—or here I am! Rosalie's 'way off talking to half a dozen folk, so I said I'd come and find our seats. Bill sent me the tickets in case we could do it."

"Where *are* you sitting? Row and number?"

Evadne glanced at the counterfoils in her hand, and looked at the rows. "Here, just on the other side of the aisle. Goody! I hoped it would be near you."

Joey laughed. "Trust Bill!—Hilda! See who's turned up! Evvy, no less—and she says Rosalie's here, too. And Evvy, Carla's behind—look! A real gathering of the clans, isn't it? Carla, you remember Evvy Lannis, of course!"

"But how could I forget?" Carla asked. "At least I could never forget the band she and Corney Flower got up. Oh, Joey, *do* you remember the concert they gave us?"

"Do I not! I laughed till I was nearly sick!" Joey gave a deep chuckle at the memory. "And they had the nerve to call on me for a solo! I suppose, Evvy, you are aware that if it hadn't been for where it was I'd have broken your necks?"

Evadne smiled complacently. "But you couldn't. We were safe enough, and we knew it. Say, Joey, I've something to show you and some news for you."

"Oh? What is it? Nice news, I hope. We've had all the horrors we want for one term."

"Very nice, thank you." Evadne looked round but no one was bothering with them at the moment. The Head was standing up to make sure that her flock were all safe, and Carla had turned to reply to a remark made to her by her next-door neighbour. Miss Lannis gave a gulp, and then thrust her left hand into Joey's lap. "Joey—look!"

Joey glanced up at her face. It wore an expression of modest pride mingled with shyness in a way that Joey, in all the years she had known Evadne, had never before seen on her face. Then she looked down at the slim hand with the diamonds flashing on the fourth finger.

"Evvy! You're engaged! Oh, I'm so glad, so very glad! Who is he? When did it happen? Tell me everything at once!"

Evadne withdrew her hand and sat down in her seat, and a little party of somewhat indignant people swept past them to find seats near the front.

"I was blocking the gangway. I knew you'd be glad, Joey."

Another bunch went past, and then Joey reiterated her demand to be told who the gentleman was. "Who is it, Evvy? You'll be Mrs—?"

"Not 'Mrs' anything!" Evadne retorted, her own woman again, now that Joey knew. "Believe it or not, Joey, I'm going to be a *Lady*!"

"If you're not already a lady," Joey said scathingly, "I'm afraid there's not much hope for you at this late date." Then her tone changed. "Lady—who?"

"He's Sir Edgar Watson and I'll be Lady Watson. He farms. And say, Joey! I'll be a stepmother! He's a widower— his first wife died seven years ago—and I'm stepping right into a ready-made family."

For a minute Joey stared at her, literally too stunned to speak. Then her golden laughter rang out. "Oh, Evvy! Not really? Well, I hope you'll be a kind stepmother to your stepchildren—or is it only one?"

"It's three—a boy and two girls. I've known him quite a while, you know—three years. We've been good friends for more than a year now, but things were only settled properly last week. And what do you mean—be a kind stepmother! I love the children dearly already. Ned—he's Edgar, after his father—is a fine boy—just twelve. And Thea and Marcia are sugarpies, both of them."

"When's the wedding to be?" Joey demanded, then added in a different tone, "Hallo! Here comes the orchestra. We'll have to pipe down now, but the first minute there is, I must hear every last detail." Then she chuckled softly while the orchestra took its places.

"What's the joke?" Evadne asked suspiciously.

"None! I was only thinking—what a thrill the school will get when they hear the very latest! Here comes Plato to conduct so we *must* dry up! But just you wait! I'm hearing everything or *else*. . . ."

With this ferocious threat, she turned to the stage as the houselights died and the footlights sprang up. The orchestra swept into a gay overture, based on the tunes of old nursery rhymes, and Evadne had to sit back and wait for the interval before they could continue their conversation.

Chapter 16

"PUSS-IN-BOOTS"

THE overture ended and when Mr. Denny had bowed in return for the storm of applause that greeted the final chord, he swung round, tapped his desk with his baton and the orchestra swept into a jolly tune which the school, at least, had no difficulty in recognising as the old Morris dance tune, *Country Gardens*. The curtain swung back to show "The Village Green" with quite a throng of people on the stage, dancing the gay old dance and singing—with some help from the wings:

> "Come, come to dancing, turning and prancing!
> Come to our May Day with song and shout!
> Laughter is ringing, all voices singing!
> Join, join our courtiers in merry rout!
>   Here is our May Queen,
>   Fair by the day seen.
> But by moonlight still fairer to see.
> When night is falling and owls are calling
> None in the land can be fairer than she!"

"I only wish I could hear the Abbess on the subject of *that* doggerel!" Mary-Lou whispered to Vi with a low chuckle. "Who on earth was responsible for it?"

"Betsy—she told me so last Sunday," Vi murmured back. "I must say it *is* rather ghastly. Writing verse isn't one of Betsy's gifts!"

"You," said Mary-Lou with emphasis, "are telling me! I'm surprised at her!"

Then the dance came to an end. The villagers whirled away from the centre of the stage to fall into picturesque groups at either side of the flower-decked chair on which sat Felicity King, a very pretty girl and prettier than ever in her May Queen's attire. Behind her stood a tall youth in baggy breeches and smock frock.

When the music died away, Felicity rose and thanked the villagers for their homage in a speech as flowery as her seat. The villagers cheered and then, from the wings, came a queer figure in Georgian attire of black, a barrister's wig a size too large, judging by his antics with it, on his head. Perched on top of the wig, was a tricorne hat and between the two, *The Lawyer* was so hot and bothered, it was a miracle that he remembered his lines.

At sight of him, however, there came a great round of clapping from the girls, for in him they recognised an old friend, Nancy Canton, who had left school the same term as it left at St. Briavel's and whom few of them had heard much of since. Above the storm of applause, Maeve Bettany's voice rose in a shriek of, "Nancy—Nancy Canton! Oh, scrummy!" which, as her own gang did not fail to tell her later, was most undignified in a girl from Va who had every reason to suppose that the next year would find her in VIb and, in all probability, a prefect!

Poor Nancy stopped dead in her progress and turned richly purple under her make-up. Then she clutched at her self-control, while the staff, scattered about among the school, hurriedly "shushed" the people nearest. The noise died down and the pantomime continued.

The tall youth came to meet this gentleman, bowing to him and saying, "Good morrow, Master Graball. I take it you are come to tell us what was my poor father's wishes with regard to his property. Pray seat yourself on this log and I will hasten to summon my brothers."

133

"Do so!" said the lawyer in an unexpectedly deep bass voice—Nancy was on the verge of wild giggles—as he scanned the property-log carefully with the aid of an enormous pair of spectacles he suddenly produced from a tail pocket and balanced on his nose, almost to the upsetting of his head-gear.

The school began to titter and the titter rose to shrieks of laughter as he picked up the tails and dusted the log with them before seating himself. "Pray return yourself if you are, as I think, one of the sons of my late lamented friend, Matthew the Miller. I recognise his nose in your face."

Fresh laughter from the audience while the young man bowed, replying, "I am Richard, his second son, commonly known as Dickon."

"Ah, quite so! Then there should be . . ." *The Lawyer* opened the enormous portfolio he carried under his arm, sorted out two or three sheets of paper of equal size and continued, "your elder brother Simon and the younger, John."

Dickon bowed again and darted off, while *The Lawyer* hotched about uncomfortably on his log in a way that caused Miss Wilson to mutter to Mlle de Lachenais sitting at her right hand, "If Nancy squirms about much more, she'll have that unfortunate log in smithereens!"

However, *Dickon* arrived before that happened, followed by *Simon* and *John*. There were no surprises here. *John* was played by tall Blossom Willoughby who made a delightful Principal Boy with her curly bob of brown hair surmounted by a green cap of the Robin Hood variety, and her lengthy legs clad beneath her green tunic in tan-coloured tights. *Simon* was Ailsa Thompson and she made a delightful contrast to the two younger brothers, for she wore a wig of straggly black locks and beard to match, and was attired in a loose garment of the dressing-gown variety in purple. Her normally pleasant face had, by means of greasepaint and lining-pencil been turned into a sour, pinched-looking one

134

and altogether, she was a most unpleasant-looking customer!

The three young men stood before *The Lawyer* who now produced from his case a document adorned with ribbons and enormous seals as he announced, "I have here your late lamented father's will."

Murmurs rose from the crowd—"Now we'll know all about it!—who's got what, I wonder?—Let's hope it doesn't all come to Simon!—Simon's a sour, mean, nasty creature—John would be the man for my money, etc."

"Well?" *Simon* grated out in a falsetto squeak. "How do things stand, eh? The mill is mine, I take it? I am the eldest son."

The Lawyer gave him a severe look. "Not so fast—not so fast, if you please!" He wrestled again with his spectacles, spread out the sheet of paper and proceeded to announce: "As you surmise, Master Simon, the mill is yours, together with the house and the land whereon both stand. Master Richard, yours is the ass, Milleton, together with his cart and all his harness, feedbags and the whip. Master John, to you, your late father leaves his black cat. Further, he bequeathes jointly to you all the following advice—or perhaps I should say one part is joined. The other is one piece of advice for each.

At this point, the spectacles tumbled off his nose and in bending to scoop them up, he lost his hat. This was an entirely unrehearsed effect and nearly brought the house down. At last he was ready and proceeded to read very impressively: "Lastly, I would wish my three said sons remember that all that glitters is not gold, and that even the finest diamond has to be cut and polished before it can sparkle; wherefore, I bid my son Simon not to be oppressive and money-grubbing; my son Richard to remember that there are more kinds of asses than one and that most of them move faster for a carrot than a whip; my son John to recall the old saying that even a cat may look at a king and why not a princess while he is about it?"

135

Having read aloud this remarkable Will, *Master Graball* proceeded to remove his glasses before he rolled up the document and held out his hand to *Simon*, demanding, "Six-and-eightpence, if you please!"

Simon grumbled loudly while he fished in each one of eight pockets and finally handed *The Lawyer* a handful of small coins. *Master Graball* carefully counted them over before he dropped them into a pocket, bowed to the brothers, the Court of the *May Queen* and, for good measure, the audience, and then turned round and began to march off. *Simon* rushed after him and caught his arm.

"Hey! Wait a bit! You haven't got my brothers' fees!"

Master Graball released himself with some dignity. "Only the chief legatee pays a fee," he said. "Good morrow to you all!" and left the stage amid loud clapping from the audience, though Vi did murmur that fairytale law seemed rather more than a little cock-eyed!

Simon raved helplessly, claiming two-and-three from each of his brothers as their share of the fee. The villagers all cried shame on him, and the *May Queen* rising from her throne announced that this ended it. Both *Simon* and *Richard* had been courting her but before she would marry such a miser as *Simon*, she would rather beg. She turned to *Dickon*, holding out her hands.

"I'll come with you and Milleton and the cart, Dickon," she said. "And when, between us, you've become a wealthy merchant, we may send our corn to Simon to be ground. Come! Let us go and seek the priest and be wed at once."

With a cry of "A wedding—a wedding!" The Villagers surrounded them and danced round them, singing to the tune of *Haste to the Wedding* another doggerel produced by Betsy Lucy, and the curtain fell on them finally forming a procession with *Dickon* and *John* leading the *May Queen*, followed by the rest while *Simon* stamped about furiously.

The next scene showed "The Mill Kitchen". Enter on the scene *Simon*, still in a towering rage. He kicked a stool out of his way and then tried to kick *The Cat* which slithered out from under him so that he staggered and nearly went head-long, just as *Dickon* and *John* entered, the former somewhat surprisingly leading *The Ass* which wagged its ears alternately, opened its mouth and gave vent to a portentous noise which bore small resemblance to a bray. Then it kicked out neatly with its right back hoof, catching *Simon* with rather more force than was intended so that the "*Ow*! he produced was very realistic. *The Ass* turned its head to look at him with such a wicked air that the audience was convulsed. *Richard* tugged it to the left and *Simon* recovering from the shock rounded on his brothers who were not backward in answering him, so that no one was surprised when he finally ordered them out of the house at once.

"Take your traps and your wretched beasts and GO!" he roared.

"What—*now*?" *Richard* asked with such incredulity in his voice that the audience giggled again. Then he added, "But we haven't had our supper."

"And you'll want it so far as I'm concerned!" *Simon* bellowed. "I've had enough of you! This place is mine and I won't have you in it! And where's the two-and-threepence you each owe me? Hand it out and be quick about it!"

Richard winked and *The Ass* followed suit. "And you've just given us the key of the open road!" its master said. "Oh, no, my fine brother! You can save it out of the supper we haven't had. You've got the mill and the house and a roof over your head and Jack and I must fish for ourselves and I've my wife to find for, too. You can count my share your wedding gift to us—a cheap one enough. Come on, Jacky! Collect your puss and we'll be off! Margery and I are for the city. We can hope to turn a penny there by using Milleton and the cart as carriers. What about you?"

"I'm for the forest," *John* replied. "At least Puss can catch rabbits and birds so we shan't starve there. You go and become a wealthy merchant. As for me—"

"As for you, to judge by what our father said, you stand a good chance of wedding a princess. Come on, Milleton! No carrots for you till you've helped to earn them. Farewell, Brother Simon. We won't forget you. When I'm a rich man maybe I'll invite you to dinner each Sunday, just to make sure you get *one* decent meal in the week."

"And I'll think about having you for a whole day on the Wednesdays," John said impressively. He turned to *The Cat* which came sidling up to him with a ridiculous effect and rubbed its head on his arm. "Good old Puss! You shall catch rabbits and I'll fish for fish for you and we'll do somehow—until that princess comes along, you know."

They made their exit, *Simon* flying after them, bawling, "Hey! I'm coming, too, to see you take naught that's mine!"

"A Wood" was the setting for the next scene, and St. Mildred's had managed well. The log from the first scene was there, and some enormous scarlet toadstools faced it with a great frog squatting on one of them. The frog, incidentally, was papier mâché and the cause of much trouble among the handcraft experts, but he looked very fine now he was done. Music stole out softly and on to the stage tripped a bevy of *Fairies*. It should have been a ballet, but most of the ballet dancers belonged to the school proper, so St. Mildred's had wisely left it to graceful movements and an airy weaving in and out and it was quite as effective as the frog and very pretty. Finally, they fell back to the sides of the stage to reveal a throne—the May Queen's throne, but now veiled in strips of many-coloured art muslin—on which sat the *Fairy Queen*— another Old Girl, Peggy Bettany, who had been in her time a most popular Head Girl. At sight of her, the combined school lost its head and yelled, "*Peggy!*" in concert.

Peggy blushed furiously. Then she rose with great dignity and sang in a charming mezzo-soprano a welcome to the fairy hall. As she finished, *Puss*, who all this time had been lying behind the log, sprang up, ran forward and knelt at her feet.

"A boon, oh, Queen—a boon!" he cried.

"Say on," *The Queen* replied in a voice nearly as silvery as Verity's.

"Grant to me the power to help my master in all things!"

"It is granted if you will pay for it," *The Queen* replied.

"I will pay. He has been good to me—to all. What is the payment?"

"Over yonder in the next country lives a wicked ogre who has vowed that he will wed the daughter of the king and so become ruler of the land. If you and your master can slay him and save the princess from so dreadful a fate, I will give you the powers you seek."

"Mistress, 'tis done!" *Puss* cried. "Give me the words of power and grant to me the gift of speaking in his own tongue that I may advise him."

The Queen raised her hand. Music stole out and the entire chorus sang softly a verse which, as it was made up of the names of all the herbs St. Mildred's could remember or find, sounded like so much gibberish to the audience. Suddenly, the stage was blacked out and when the lights came back, it was to a moonlight effect. The throne had vanished, and curled up beneath the toadstools was *John*, apparently sound asleep. *The Cat* came bounding on and proceeded to rouse him by taking its tail and brushing his face with the end until he sat up, yawning and stretching.

"Hello, Cat!" he said as he got to his feet. "Where have you been?"

"To visit a friend of mine—and yours," *Puss* replied.

John jumped and set the toadstools rocking, whereupon a voice from the wings was distinctly heard by the front rows of the audience to exclaim, "Oh, bother Blossom! I *warned* her not to stand too near!"

"But—but you can talk! *John* exclaimed.

"Certainly, if I wish to do so," *Puss* replied haughtily.

"Then why did you never do it before? Though on the whole, I'm thankful you didn't. That beautiful elder brother of mine would certainly never have let me have you if he had heard you. He would have kicked me out into the world alone and sold you to some circus for every penny he could squeeze out of the proprietor."

"Have no fear!" *Puss* replied. "He would never have heard me. I have not forgotten how he tried to kick me and grudged me even a spoonful of milk when he saw you give it to me from your own mug. Master, you have been good to me ever since you rescued me from the millpool where Simon threw me when I was a kitten. Now it is my turn. Only promise me to do exactly as I say and I will promise you great happiness and fortune."

"I don't see how you can manage that. We shan't make much of a fortune, even if we sell every rabbit you catch. As for happiness; wealth doesn't mean that always."

Puss squatted down before him. "Tell me, Master, what makes happiness?"

The orchestra was quick on its cue. It broke into a lilting air and *John* sang a charming song with which Betsy Lucy had had nothing to do, in which he declared that happiness lay in love and love only.

When he had finished, *Puss* said, "I can promise you love as well as wealth. Only promise to do as I ask."

"Very well. I promise. What is your first wish, Puss?"

"Go into the town at the further end of this wood and buy me a pair of boots."

"*Boots*?" *John* goggled at him. "Oh, very well. Anything else? I have precious little money, you know, and we've got to find food and a bed yet."

"Bring me the boots and a large bag with a draw-string and leave the rest to me," *Puss* returned.

"You're the boss," *John* responded slangily. "I shan't be long."

He made his exit and then *The Ass* rather unexpectedly turned up and the pair proceeded to perform a burlesque of the Fan Gavotte which nearly brought the house down. Then

140

The Ass clattered off as *John* arrived with a pair of top-boots in one hand and an enormous sack in the other. He handed them to *Puss* who sat on the log, tugged on the boots and then, throwing the sack over his shoulder, walked off calling, "Wait here, Master. I shall be back ere long."

John turned to stare after him, scratching his head in a bewildered fashion before he sat on the log with great caution and proceeded to warble a ballad about a fair maiden behind a hedge who met a poor shepherd. They fell in love, but, it seemed in vain until her swain flung off his disguise and stood revealed as the lord of the manor. By the time it was finished, *Puss* came bounding in to throw a small jingling bag at his master's feet.

"Lo, Master," he said, "I caught six hares in my sack and took them to the palace in the next country where the head cook bought them for five crowns. Now we shall fare well. Furthermore, the next I catch shall be a gift to the king himself from the Marquis of Carrabas."

"From who?" *John* demanded.

"From you, Master. That is your title. Ere long, you shall own a castle and broad lands and have many servants and labourers to till your lands. But do as I say and all will be yours—even the love you so greatly desire. But we must not tarry here. By dawn tomorrow, we must have entered the next country where all awaits you. Come, let us set forth. When we are there, we have to kill an ogre, you and I."

"Kill a what?" *John* gasped.

"An ogre, Master, that means to marry the king's only daughter, a damsel as fair as the day and as good as she is beautiful. Would you not dare everything to save such a lady from so fearful a fate?"

"Aye, indeed. Lead on, Puss! As for the ogre, I'll do my best or die in the attempt!"

"No need of that, Master. And when he is dead, all that is now his will be yours and you will free the land from his wicked sway and," *Puss* wound up with startling effect, "all will be gas and gaiters!"

The pair turned and as they did so, the curtains fell and the first act was over!

Chapter 17

THE END OF THE PANTOMIME

As the house lights sprang up, those of the Seniors responsible for the refreshments left their seats and scurried off to the side-rooms, where trays of tea, coffee, tubs of ices and sweets and chocolate awaited them. They distributed their wares quickly and efficiently and had time to have a hot drink themselves before they collected the cups.

They had just finished when the house lights went down and the footlights blazed again. The orchestra had come in and were taking their places, and a moment later a stately minuet rang out, and the curtains went up on the court of *King Amyas of Catmalania* to show court ladies and gentlemen dancing the minuet. *The King* sat on his throne, looking very stately in white Georgian suit and crimson mantle, but even his wig and the magnificent crown pressed down on it could not disguise Clem Barras, a much-loved Old Girl whose schooldays had ended only two years before. When his Majesty rose as the dance ended and the dancers swung across the stage to the sides with much billowing of panniers and coat-tails, the school broke into tumultuous clapping.

Warned by what had happened to Peggy, Clem lost not a whit of her self-possession. She stood waiting until the clapping died down, then took a cautious step forward, and announced: "My people! I take this opportunity to make it known that I have decided it is high time we were relieved of the presence of the wicked ogre who has taken up his abode in the borders of our land and is robbing us of our people to

143

make them into mutton pies. It is our design to offer lands, wealth and the hand of our daughter, our only child and heiress, to him who shall slay this monster and so free the land from him."

At this point every light in the place winked violently and went out—even the guidelights at the back and sides of the auditorium. There was a loud gasp from the audience, and a voice rose in a howl—a voice that Joey recognised with an awful qualm. Felix was startled and frightened, and when that happened, he yelled. What was worse, his twin always copied him. Sure enough, a second howl rose as a voice from the stage exclaimed, "Please keep your seats! It's all right!"

Close on the heels of this came another voice. "Twins! Shut up at once! It's only the light failed for a moment. Oh, somebody, smother them—quick!" Despite her anxiety, Joey chuckled. She recognised Maeve's voice.

Evidently someone did do something about it, for the howls died down fairly quickly, and at that moment the lights blazed forth again. The actors had been well-drilled and not one of them had moved, though the shock of the sudden darkness had caused *The King* to jerk so violently that his crown was cocked over his left ear. He calmly put up a hand and straightened it, and he went on with his speech.

He called on *The Princess* to ratify his statement, and she came forward. Sybil Russell was a lovely girl, and she looked even lovelier than usual in her court dress. She spoke the few lines given her in a very sweet, clear voice that reached to the back of the hall. When she sat down again, the doors at the side were flung open, and a tall footman announced in tones that were nearly suffocated with laughter, "An emissary from the Marquis of Carabas with a gift for your Majesty."

The girls recognised yet another of the Bettanys—Bride—and there had to be a brief pause to allow the girls to express their delight at seeing her again. Then *Puss* bustled in with an invitation to *His Majesty* and *Her Royal Highness* to take dinner next day with the most noble, the Marquis of Carrabas.

The King read it aloud to the assembled company, and then turned to *Puss*. "The Marquis, your master, is indeed generous. He has loaded us with gifts of fresh game, delicious wild fruits, and such flowers as we have not known before. Upon my word, Sir Puss—"

Out went the lights, and *The King* was left to continue his speech in the darkness, which he did with great firmness, thus saving a second outbreak of woe from the twins. The rest of the cast followed his example, giving, as Joey remarked over Cecil's head to Evadne, the effect of a radio programme. By the time they came on again, the scene had changed to an attic where *John*, judging by his speech, was spending his days with much boredom, though he still retained his trust in *Puss*. Enter to him his *Landlady* to demand the rent—which he had not got. She held forth with much vigour on the iniquity of lodgers who expected to be housed and fed, never to speak of keeping a great, nasty cat, and all for nothing! *John* replied to her with much dignity that she would have her money all in good time, but that was no use. She wanted it then, and she hustled in her husband—an enormously tubby man—to back her up.

The three went at it hammer and tongs, and the audience were in fits of laughter, especially as they all talked at cross-purposes and interrupted each other regardless. It ended when *Puss* stalked in and proceeded to empty a bag of tin money all over the stage and bid the couple take their rent and go. Both crawled about on all fours, after the coins, while *Puss* and *John* watched, making remarks and pointing out gleaming silvery circlets they had missed. One had rolled into a corner, and the old man with an entirely unrehearsed effect, gasped, "If I stand on my head, I'll get it!" and promptly elevated his heels, stunning his fellow actors into startled silence before he completed a neat somersault and turned right side up again.

At this point, several people wept gently, and Mary-Lou uttered a strangled whoop as *Puss*, in very shaky tones, spoke his lines. As for *The Landlady*, she remained sitting on the floor, gaping at her agile spouse until *John*, who had edged nearer, poked her with his foot when she remembered her speech and gave it—very flatly.

There came a roar of cheering and laughter when the curtains fell. And that is to be taken literally. For some reason they stuck halfway. The two people responsible tugged violently, and the wire-rope snapped with a loud twang! The curtains collapsed, completely obliterating *Puss*, who squawked loudly. And that was where the lights, having kept everyone on tenderhooks for the whole of the latter part of the performance, expired finally. There had been a failure at the power station, and the entire district was blacked out.

There was nothing to be done but to end the show. The orchestra stood, and, with a good many false notes since they were playing in the light of two torches someone had produced, played the National Anthem, and the pantomime was over.

"And to think they still have full daylight in the valley!" Mary-Lou groaned as she helped to organise the return of the school in the various cars that had been put at their service. "Oh, I know it's not pitch dark up here yet, but it's dusk. Are we to see the Old Girls, does anyone know?"

No one did; but it gradually leaked out that those ladies were staying up at the Platz until the next day when they expected to leave by the same train as the school.

"If it's running!" Hilary said forebodingly.

"What do you mean—if it's running?" Vi demanded as the prefects, having obtained leave to walk back, since every vehicle was packed, set off.

"Well, what about the railway? It goes by electricity, doesn't it? If it's off, too, will you tell me how we're going to get down tomorrow? We can't walk all that way *and* carry our cases!"

The entire body stood stockstill at this awful thought. They had forgotten about the railway. And the road was still closed to wheeled traffic, so that was no help, either.

Clare moaned loudly. "There's been a hoodoo on this term! I'm convinced of it! Never, since I've been at school, have there been so many awful happenings!"

"And what about our people?" Josette cried. "They'll be expecting us at home the day after tomorrow. If we can't get down tomorrow we shan't be at home till the end of the week!"

Mary-Lou called them to order. "If it comes to *that*, the Abbess will let them know somehow—if it means sending people down to cable from Interlaken. Meanwhile, may I remind you that Kaffee und Kuchen will be waiting, and there won't be a prefect in the place? Come on! Besides," she added plaintively, "I'm hungry!"

"She's right," Hilary Bennet said. "Come on, folks! Best foot forward! Tonight, we have Spot Supper, remember, and even if we don't go home tomorrow, we'll certainly get off next day, and all will be well."

But when they reached the school, they found that Fate had reserved the worst blow of all till then. Naomi had been packed off in a motor-cycle combination belonging to one of the young doctors, for she was very tired. Just at the bend in the road before the school, he had skidded and she had been flung out against a big boulder. The Maynards' car had been just behind, mercifully, and Jack Maynard, driving, had braked instantly, nearly entering a skid himself, and leapt out. The doctor himself was shaken and bruised, but Naomi was concussed and they were afraid of internal injury. Dr. Maynard had lifted Naomi into his car, and gone, hell-for-leather, back along the road to the Sanatorium. Now, permission or no permission, Naomi already lay on the table in the operating theatre where the doctors were at work on her, performing a long and difficult major operation, since, if it was not done at once, she must die.

Chapter 18

Happy Ending

"Is there any news yet? Have any of you heard?" Verity Carey, bringing a message from the Head to the prefects, asked anxiously.

"Not a thing," Hilary replied. "Perhaps there's news now, though, and that's why the Head's sent for us."

It was nearly nineteen o'clock, and the Seniors, at any rate, all knew what news might come from the great Sanatorium. It was no part of the Chalet School training to shield the elder girls from all sorrow. The great aim was to turn them into strong, helpful, reliable women. When Joey had brought the first news the Head had said instantly that Naomi's own clan must hear.

The prefects left their room in a body. They had kept together most of the time since the news had come, feeling comfort from each other. The Head was in her drawing room, and when they arrived, she lifted a strained face which made Mary-Lou run forward to kneel beside her. "Miss Annersley! It wasn't *your* fault!" she cried. "I know you've got the responsibility, but please, *please* don't look like that! Naomi is stronger than she was when she first came, and—and we've all been praying that she may come through. And even—even if she—she doesn't, she'll have gone to join her father and mother, so it will be all right for her!"

The Head put her gently to one side. "Thank you, Mary-Lou. I know all that, child; but, as you say, the responsibility is mine in the end. Find seats, all of you. I want to speak to you about Spot Supper."

"Oh, we can't possibly have it now!" Vi burst out. "Not all that row and singing when—when—"

"But that is just what you must do," Miss Annersley said gravely. "Oh, not the speeches! I agree that that would be asking too much of us just now. But the meal is ready and must be eaten. And we can't think of ourselves only. There are the younger girls. They know that Naomi has met with an accident, but we haven't told them the worst as we have you Seniors. We must have our singing and carry on as nearly as we can for their sakes."

The prefects looked at each other. How could they do it?

Miss Annersley leaned back in her chair, her eyes going from one grave young face to another. "I know it seems impossible," she said quietly. "All the same, I want you to do your best. Furthermore, it is what Naomi herself would wish, I know. She wouldn't want the last day of term spoiled for the younger girls for her sake. Naomi is stronger in very many more ways than in health, you know. She has been learning to think for others, and she would be very sorry to think that the little girls were deprived of their usual fun because she was hurt. I know it seems a lot to ask of you, but in the years to come, you may have to face trials as bad or even worse than this." Then she added what proved the turning-point for the most doubtful of them. "I am prepared to do my part. Will you do yours?"

One by one, after a little pause, they agreed to do their best. She nodded.

"I thought you would. Thank you, girls. Then the gong will sound shortly, and though I think we'll omit the usual procession, we'll go to Abendessen and not hurt Karen's feelings by rejecting the feast she has planned for us."

"Is there any news, Miss Annersley?" Hilda Jukes asked.

"Not yet. But if Naomi comes through it they hope that much of her lameness will be relieved and she will be stronger than she has been since the accident. It will be a long convalescence for her, but if she pulls through, it will be to a much fuller life than she has known for more than six years."

"Does her aunt know?" Mary-Lou asked.

"I cabled her at once, but I don't think she will have got it yet."

"Then—then is she alone?"

"No. Joey Maynard has gone to be with her."

Lesley Bethune gave a sigh of relief. "Oh, I'm so glad! Mrs. Maynard can be just like one of us, but—"

Prunella took the words out of her mouth. "I know. When she likes she can be nothing but a *mother*. She was that to me, years ago, and I'll never forget it. Even if her aunt can't come Naomi will have all the mothering anyone could want."

"Quite all right, Prunella. Now, will you all go and get ready for Abendessen? Some of you look wild and all of you could do with a wash. You'll feel better for it." The Head rose to her feet, and they knew it was dismissal. They filed quietly out of the room and went to obey her. But when she was alone for a moment with Hilary and Vi, Mary-Lou said thoughtfully, "Did you notice the Head's hair? *I* did. The lamplight caught it, and there were white hairs in it. I've never noticed them before."

"We've got to back her to the limit," Vi said with conviction. "Come on! I mean to eat my share. We can't give her a single worry more, and, you know, she *will* worry if she thinks we're grizzling or being miserable."

"It's a bargain!" Hilary said. "I'll do likewise."

"And so will I!" Mary-Lou turned. "Time we were turfing out the kids from their common rooms. Let's get cracking!"

So Spot Supper was held, though without the noise that usually accompanied it. The only speech made was the Head's. When the meal was ended, she stood up, and the girls turned to the high table at once, eager to know if news had come from the Sanatorium. She guessed it and shook her head.

"No, girls. I have no news for you yet, and do not expect to have any for at least another hour. You shall know as soon as it comes. Meanwhile, we will have a sing-song for an hour, and after that, Prayers and then bed. As you can see for yourselves, the electricity is still off. It is unlikely that you can get off early in the morning as we all expected; but I have contacted the authorities, and they say they hope to have the railway running again some time tomorrow. Postcards have been sent to all your people to tell them what has happened, so they won't worry about you. Now I want you to go to Hall where we will have a sing-song until Prayers. Stand! Turn! Forward—*march*!"

As one girl the school marched out. Most of the staff went with them, but two or three of the younger mistresses remained behind to clear the tables, and the Head went to the study to ring up the Sanatorium and ask if there was any news. There was none, and she had to join the school with an anxious heart.

Sing-song was quieter than usual. With one accord they let the usual shouting songs like "Fhairshon" and "October" alone. But they had "Drink to me only" and "Golden Slumbers", "Cherry Ripe" and "The Lark in the Morn", and a good many others of the same kind. When the hour ended, they had Prayers and many were the silent prayers that went up for Naomi just as she was laid in the high white bed, safely through the operation itself, though no one could yet say how she would stand up to the shock.

Jack Maynard himself rang up the school when it was all over, and gave the news to a Head surrounded by her full staff.

"She's come through so far, but it's going to be touch and go with her. I'm staying here all night, and so is Joey in case she rouses. At present, she's still under the anaesthetic. There's one thing, Hilda. If she does come through she'll be almost normal. But you won't get her back for a long time. It's going to mean a long convalescence. She isn't Mary-Lou, you know! And we had to do a lot—three ribs badly broken and a piece of bone to remove from the skull, besides minor injuries. But at least she's past the first stage. Now I must go. Joey will stay for the present, but I hope to get her home tomorrow. It'll mean drugs for the first day or two, so it'll make no difference to Naomi then. Goodnight."

So the Head was able to go round the dormitories and tell all those awake that the operation had been successful. It satisfied most of the girls, who promptly thought that Naomi would soon be better. But Vi was a doctor's niece and Lesley Bethune and Josette Russell doctors' daughters. They knew that it was still not certain. So did Mary-Lou when Miss Annersley appeared in the little room which was hers by virtue of being Head Girl. She was in bed but not asleep, and she sat up at once when the light of the big torch glowed through the opening door.

"I'm awake, Miss Annersley. Is there—is there any news?" she asked.

"Yes, and it's good news. Naomi has come safely through the operation."

Mary-Lou nodded. "How is she after it?"

"No one can say yet. It's too soon. But at least she is through."

"Well," said Mary-Lou with the stunning assurance that was a characteristic of hers, "that means that she's still in grave danger, doesn't it? I mean, I've heard Uncle Jack and Uncle Jem talking, and you've got to face the shock of it all."

"Yes; there is that," the Head assented, wishing inwardly that the two doctors had held their tongues before a quick girl like Mary-Lou. "But the news is good so far, Mary-Lou. Be thankful for that, and lie down and go to sleep."

Mary-Lou nodded again. "I will if I can—go to sleep, I mean. Oh, I hope she'll come through! Miss Annersley!"

"Yes?" the Head said, wondering what was coming next.

"She may need blood transfusions. If she does, and if mine's all right, may I be the one to give it to her?"

Miss Annersley gasped. "No; you may *not!*" she said firmly when she got her breath back. "For one thing, you're too young. For another, they have all the plasma they want at the San. Now stop talking, and go to sleep. I hope and I believe that the news in the morning will be better. But we must wait for that."

"OK." Mary-Lou snuggled down. "But you'll let us know as soon as there is any, won't you?"

"As soon as I know myself. I'm going. Goodnight, Mary-Lou. God bless you, child." Miss Annersley got herself out of the room—the last of all she had to visit—but when she finally reached the study again, she flung herself into the nearest chair and went off into such a peal of laughter as made the startled staff seriously wonder if she had become hysterical from the strain.

She pushed them away as they thronged round her, and, still laughing, repeated Mary-Lou's amazing offer to them. They heard her, thunderstruck. Then little Miss Andrews began to giggle, and before long they were all laughing.

"But oh, how like Mary-Lou!" Mdlle exclaimed, mopping her eyes. "She is always ready, n'est-ce pas?"

"Rather too ready this time, if you ask me!" Nancy Wilmot rejoined. "But you've said it, Jeanne—it is, just exactly, Mary-Lou; I can say no more!"

"Well, I certainly never expected to end this day with a burst of laughter," Miss Annersley said as she stood up. "I fancy there is coffee for us in the drawing room. Shall we go and see? And then, I think we had better go to bed. It has been a long day for us all, and these last hours have been terrible. Please God, the worst is over now. Somehow, I feel that Naomi will pull through."

Next morning, Jack Maynard rang up the school at seven o'clock to say that, although no one could speak with any certainty as yet, so far Naomi was holding her own.

Shortly after came the news that the railway would be open again by sixteen o'clock that afternoon, so the girls would be able to leave that day after all. Announcing this after Prayers, the Head told them that they would spend the

153

morning in going for walks. Mittagessen would be at thirteen o'clock, and Dr. Jack had promised to ring up at fifteen so that they should hear the very latest news before they went home. Then she shooed them all off to get ready for their walk, and told them to take biscuits with them as they were to be out most of the morning. Leaving at so late an hour would mean the night train to Paris, and she meant them to sleep through as much of the journey as possible.

The prefects held a consultation as soon as Mittagesen was over—a somewhat scrappy Mittagessen, since no one had expected the school to be still at the Görnetz Platz by that time—and when, at fifteen o'clock the bell rang to summon them to Hall, they had a plan prepared.

Miss Annersley held Prayers first. Then the door opened, when the Catholic contingent had returned to Hall and Joey Maynard mounted the dais. She looked very tired, but there was triumph in her face as she came forward to the reading desk.

"Girls!" she said, "the good news holds! Naomi is still making progress, even though it is almost infinitesimal. But the doctors all agree that her hold on life is stronger than it was last night. She is still in danger—don't think *that* is over yet. It won't be for some days. Dr. Jack told me to tell you that if this goes on,—by the time you come back for the summer term she will be well enough to have visits from you all. And another thing! During last night's operation they were able to put right something that has been wrong ever since her first accident. When she is able to move about again, her lameness will be much better and she will be much straighter."

She was about to step back, but Mary-Lou jumped to her feet and checked her with a ringing call of, "Auntie Joey!"

Joey stopped and looked at her. "Well, what now?"

"Just this. We all want to know how Naomi goes on, of course, but no one could write to even all us Seniors—too much work, altogether. So we prefects have made a collection—I'll give it to you in a minute—and would you please send a notice each week, to one of the big dailies, just to tell us how she is?"

Joey forgot that she was Mrs. Maynard. "Gosh!" she exclaimed. "What *will* you folk think of next?" Then she grinned. "Not that it isn't a good idea. Hand the cash over, and I'll be personally responsible for it. I'll put it in *The Times* and head it 'Naomi'. Look down the Personal column and you'll soon find it."

Joey kept her word, and twice each week during the holidays notices appeared which told them that all was going well and Naomi, having started to cling to life, was gripping it with a tenacious hold. On the Monday of the second week, when Mary-Lou and Verity were staying at the Lucys' with Vi, she read the last one aloud at the breakfast table.

"Naomi recovering steadily. All well."

"Good!" said Mrs. Lucy with a smile at the joyful faces.

Mary-Lou removed the paper from Vi's grasp and read it to herself. She looked up. "Well, no one could say last term was peaceful in the slightest degree. In fact, I never remember a term so full of the most ghastly trials before. But this makes up for a lot. And the greatest beauty of it all is that, thanks to the accident, Naomi will be more or less all right and that's something that might never have happened otherwise. Good for the Chalet School!"

A Fresh Wind in the Willows
by Dixon Scott

Toad takes up cricket . . . Mole goes ballooning . . . Rat builds an ark . . . Badger teaches bell ringing

The enchanting world of the Riverbank lives on in this affectionate sequel to *The Wind in the Willows*. Here are your favourite characters in a new series of delightful adventures, written by a life-long admirer of Kenneth Grahame's masterpiece.

"Scott's characters and writing capture the style and flavour of the original superbly."   *Daily Mirror*

"It has captured the atmosphere of the original beautifully."   *Daily Express*

"Charming . . . sunlit . . . engaging illustrations."
Sunday Express

Armada

'JINNY' BOOKS
by Patricia Leitch

FOR LOVE OF A HORSE
When Jinny Manders rescues Shantih, a chestnut Arab, from a cruel circus, her dream of owning a horse seems to come true. But Shantih escapes on to the moors.

A DEVIL TO RIDE
Shantih, safe at last, is inseparable from Jinny. But the Arab is impossible to ride.

THE SUMMER RIDERS
Jinny is furious when Marlene, a city girl, comes to stay. But when Marlene's brother gets into trouble with the police, only Jinny and Shantih can help him.

NIGHT OF THE RED HORSE
When archaeologists excavate an ancient site, Jinny and Shantih fall under the terrifying power of the Celtic 'Pony Folk'.

GALLOP TO THE HILLS
When Ken Dawson's dog, Kelly, is wrongly accused of killing sheep, Jinny is determined to save him. But will she be in time?

HORSE IN A MILLION
Jinny is heart-broken when Shantih disappears one night. Desperate to find her, Jinny begins a dangerous search.

THE MAGIC PONY
Jinny's life is full of problems when she rescues an aged white pony. But an ancient magic intervenes.

RIDE LIKE THE WIND
Finmory House is to be sold, and Jinny and Shantih must go back to the city. How can Jinny save the home she loves?

Armada

GOOD WIVES

Louisa M. Alcott

As the four March sisters grow up, their lives lead them in very different directions.

Amy travels the Continent, and Meg settles down to a marriage that is not quite the continual paradise she imagined. Beth, with the secret she tried so hard to hide, stays at home, whilst Jo makes a bold bid for fame and fortune in New York – an adventure which changes the whole course of her life . . .

GOOD WIVES continues the story of the heart-warming March family, begun in LITTLE WOMEN.

First Steps with your Spectrum

A Beginner's Guide to Programming

by Carolyn Hughes

This book takes you step by step from your first tap at the keyboard to writing your own Spectrum programs.

DISCOVER how to use colour and sound
MAKE objects move about the screen
LEARN BASIC programming techniques
IMPROVE your skills with specially written programs

PLUS six exciting games programs, including *Morse Mole*, *Mind Reader* and *Alien*.

". . .eases the earliest beginner into BASIC comfortingly and successfully." *Guardian*
". . .concise and lucid explanations." *T.E.S.*

FONTANA PAPERBACKS

HI KIDS! I'VE GOT THE POWER TO BRING YOU FUN, ADVENTURE, AND EXCITEMENT!

Here are just a few of the best-selling titles that Armada has to offer:

- ☐ The Castle of Darkness *J.H. Brennan* £1.50
- ☐ Anyone Can Draw *Introduced by Tony Hart* £1.25
- ☐ The Funniest Funbook *Edited by Mary Danby* £1.25
- ☐ What Katy Did *Susan M. Coolidge* 95p
- ☐ A Fresh Wind in the Willows *Dixon Scott* £1.25
- ☐ Ten Ponies & Jackie *Judith M. Berrisford* £1.25
- ☐ The Mystery of the Scar-Faced Beggar
  Three Investigators Series £1.25
- ☐ The Emperor's Pony *Ann Sheldon* £1.25
- ☐ The Wizard of Oz *L. Frank Baum* 95p
- ☐ Little Men *Louisa M. Alcott* £1.25
- ☐ Shadow the Sheepdog *Enid Blyton* £1.25

Armadas are available in bookshops and newsagents, but can also be ordered by post.

HOW TO ORDER
ARMADA BOOKS, Cash Sales Dept., GPO Box 29, Douglas, Isle of Man. British Isles. Please send purchase price plus 15p per book (maximum postal charge £3·00). Customers outside the UK also send purchase price plus 15p per book. Cheque, postal or money order — no currency.

NAME (Block letters) _____

ADDRESS _____

_____

_____